S0-AAD-951

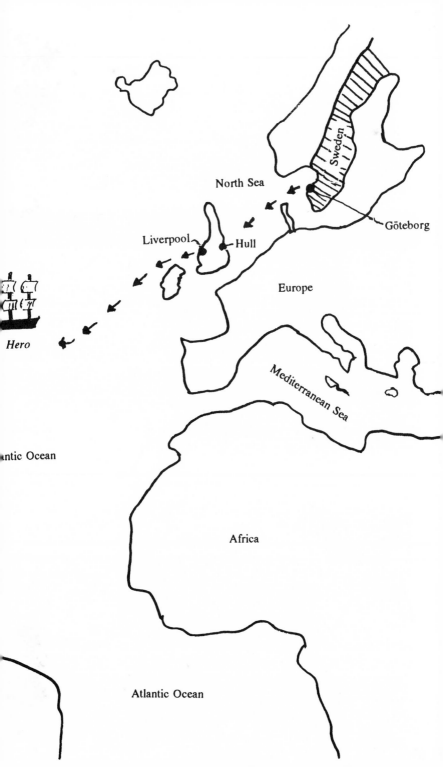

Hero

North Sea

Sweden

Göteborg

Liverpool

Hull

Europe

Mediterranean Sea

Atlantic Ocean

Africa

Atlantic Ocean

A Swedish Boy In Early Texas

HEJ TEXAS
Goodbye
SWEDEN

SAMMYE MUNSON
AUTHOR OF OUR TEJANO HEROES

EAKIN PRESS ★ AUSTIN, TEXAS

FIRST EDITION

Copyright © 1994
By Sammye Munson

Published in the United States of America
By Eakin Press
An Imprint of Sunbelt Media, Inc.
P.O. Drawer 90159 ★ Austin, TX 78709-0159

ALL RIGHTS RESERVED. No part of this book may be repro-
duced in any form without written permission from the publisher,
except for brief passages included in a review appearing in a
newspaper or magazine.

ISBN 0-89015-948-3

Library of Congress Cataloging-in-Publication Data

Munson, Sammye.
    Goodye, Sweden, hej Texas / by Sammye Munson.
        p.   cm.
    Summary: In 1880 fifteen-year-old Carl Olsson leaves Sweden to work on his
brother's farm in Texas.
    ISBN 0-89015-948-3 : $12.95
    [1. Swedish Americans–Fiction. 2. Texas–Fiction. 3. Emigration and immi-
gration–Fiction. 4. Farm life–Texas–Fiction.]
I. Title.
PZ7.M9275Go   1994
[Fic]–dc20   93-38928
                                                                          CIP
                                                                           AC

For these Swedish Americans
dear to my heart:
Leslie, David, Mark, Paul,
Christopher, and Matthew

This book is fiction but was inspired by the life of Claus Munson, who came to Texas as a fifteen-year-old in 1880 and might have had the same experiences as Carl.

Contents

CHAPTER I

Southern Sweden, 1880

"You're late coming home," Papa said gruffly.

"I stopped to skate on the Peterson pond," Carl explained.

"You're fifteen now," Papa reminded him. "You're no longer a boy who can play whenever he pleases."

"Papa, what's the matter?" Carl asked, taking off his worn boots and warming himself at the fireplace.

"I must talk to you like a man. It is hard to say this, but I must. Our farm does not make enough money for us to live. You have to quit school and get a job."

"You mean quit school forever or just for awhile?"

Papa's face looked old and worried. His brow was wrinkled. "I don't know," he said softly. Then he looked into Carl's eyes and when he spoke again, his voice was full of certainty. "You know how poor the crops have been. The drought has gone on for four years. They predict it will continue. We can't grow enough food to eat or wheat to sell."

"I'll work harder, Papa," Carl pleaded. "I'll work on the farm every afternoon and on weekends."

"That won't make a difference. I know you like school,

and you're a good *studerande*. But we need help on the farm. It is too small to support two families. When your brother, Pelle, got married, he inherited half the farm. That is the Swedish custom."

Carl stared at his father, his lips pursed. He didn't understand the Swedish tradition that gave half the family farm to the eldest son. It wasn't fair. Why couldn't he have been born first?

"Look at your boots. They have big holes in them. I can't even afford to buy you decent boots," Papa said.

"That can wait. It's not important," Carl said.

He thought about his other brother, Oscar, who went to America four years ago. Oscar knew that Pelle would inherit half the farm. He also knew that the farm was too small to be divided again. So, he decided to leave.

"I've thought about this a long time, Carl. You must get a job. I hear that the spool factory is hiring. It's a five mile walk from here. But you're strong. You can walk," Papa said as he lit his pipe and rubbed a finger across his forehead as if to erase the worry lines. He regarded Carl with solemn eyes and said, "Many boys your age are already working."

Carl could not look at Papa. Instead, he stared at the roaring fire, feeling the heat on his face and body. Yes, other boys his age worked. But he had hoped to attend school until he turned sixteen.

Mama walked in at that moment, her wool hat pulled over her forehead, her face red and chapped from the cold. Carl remembered, not too many years ago, when everyone thought she was pretty. But that was when times were not so hard.

"Ah, snow again. I'm glad you're home, Carl," she said.

"Mama, I'll take the bucket of milk to the kitchen. I would have milked Vesty for you," Carl said.

"It's my job, milking the cows. I don't mind."

As Carl took the bucket to the kitchen, he saw little Axelina. She ran to him and tugged at his trousers.

"I don't have time to play now," he told his six-year-old sister. I'm have to check on the oxen."

The child looked surprised that her brother was so abrupt. But Carl wasn't in any mood to play with her. He needed to be alone and think about Papa's words. Suddenly his entire life was changing. What would his future hold? He couldn't go to school or even work on the family farm. He imagined being buried in the walls of the spool factory forever.

Outside in the snow, he tripped on one of the many rocks on their farm. He kicked it hard, trying to rid himself of the hurt and anger he felt toward Papa, the Swedish ways, and the thin, rocky soil that covered the Swedish earth.

The silent falling of the snowflakes blanketed the ground in white. Carl's boots made deep tracks in the snow. He walked without direction in the cold, dark evening. Looking up at the black sky, he wished for a miracle.

The brisk winter wind blew his blonde hair in all directions. But he didn't feel the chill, only a deep disappointment in his heart.

Carl fed the oxen, then made his way to the house, half-frozen, his feet numb. When he opened the door, he smelled the wonderful aroma of newly-baked bread. But, not even Mama's bread could lift his spirits.

The conversation with Papa still haunted him. The thought of leaving school to work in the spool factory was so painful that he couldn't speak of it. He wanted to beat his fists against a wall.

Early the next morning, he dressed warmly and walked five miles to the spool factory. He was hired at once and began work in a large, noisy room full of machinery. His job was to trim and smooth logs to be used in making large wooden spools for weaving and spinning.

Carl's job was not difficult, but it was boring. The room where he worked had no windows and little heat. He kept his coat on as he worked. When he walked home that evening, the sky was completely dark.

Nearing his house, he saw a lone oil lamp in the window. Smoke coming from the chimney cheered him. Inside, he took off his wet boots and warmed his feet at the fire-place. How good it was to be home.

As he began to feel warm, he looked up to see Christina, his older sister. Her golden hair fell to her shoulders, and her blue eyes met his.

"Ah, *Bror*, you look half-frozen. Here, take a cup of hot tea," she said.

"*Tack så mycket*, Christina."

His eyes were full of gratitude for his sister. Four years older than he, she always was the caring big sister.

"So, how was work at the *fabrik*?" she asked curiously.

"Not so bad. But it was noisy, cold, and boring."

Christina laughed out loud. "Sounds wonderful. Maybe I could work there, too, and we could freeze together," she teased.

"The factory doesn't hire women," Carl said flatly.

"That's typical. There are no jobs for women in all of Sweden. When can I ever go to Texas and join my boyfriend Henning?"

"Henning promised to buy your ticket when he earned the money," Carl reminded her.

"That could be a year or two. I might be an old woman before I get to Texas. And Henning may marry someone else."

"I don't think so," Carl consoled her. "He promised he'd wait for you."

"Yes, but waiting can be difficult. If there was only some way I could earn money, I could help. I'm not lazy. I could do many things," she said.

"You just have to be patient."

"You don't know how it is to love someone and be thousands of miles away from him."

"Henning would be foolish not to wait for you," Carl said reassuringly.

"You're saying that because you're my brother. Come into the kitchen. I need to help Mama with supper."

Mama was stirring a big pot as they walked into the

5

kitchen. "You'll both feel better after you've eaten a good, hot meal," Mama said.

"I sure am hungry. What are we having to eat tonight?" Carl asked.

"Pork and potatoes," Mama said, wiping her hands on her apron.

"Again?" Carl asked in a teasing voice.

"*Ja,* and if we didn't raise hogs, we wouldn't have any meat at all," Christina said.

"Thanks be to God for hogs," Mama added, a twinkle in her tired eyes.

"Sweden is the land of beauty, the land of lakes, but why is the soil beneath the grass so thin and rocky?" Carl asked, tasting the stew.

"It was always thin, rocky soil, not fit for anything except to look at," Mama said, shaking her apron.

"We can't even grow enough potatoes to last a winter," added Christina.

At that moment, little Axelina rushed in from the other room. "Lena's uncle is going to America! Can we go, too?" she shouted.

Mama laughed. "Everybody wants to go to America. Is it so much better there?" She shook her head and said, "I don't think so. No, *flicka,* we aren't going to America."

"Oscar has been in Texas for four years now. I wonder what he looks like," Carl remarked, staring outside and trying to picture his older brother.

Mama called Papa from the other room. "Show him the letter, Papa."

With some hesitation, Papa took an envelope from his vest. He held it a moment, then handed it to Carl.

"You might as well read it," he said.

A glance at the envelope told Carl the letter was from Oscar. He began reading aloud:

My Dear family,

I hope that you are well. We lead busy lives on the farm. Crops such as corn, oats, and cotton grow well here in this rich, black soil. I cannot keep up with the work. If Carl wants to come to Texas, I will help him. He must think about this carefully and make a decision. My wife, Ingrid, and little Erik send their love.

Your son and brother,
Oscar

Carl reread the letter, making sure he understood his brother's meaning. Was Oscar offering to pay his passage to America? Carl remembered his father's words: the farm could not support two families. Should he go to Texas? He read the letter again, then put it back in the envelope and looked at his family.

Tears began to form in his mother's eyes. *How does she always know what I'm thinking?* he wondered. He put his arm around her.

"Don't make a hasty decision," Mama said. "The crops may improve this year. We may have rain."

"It won't matter, Mama," Carl said. "Pelle has half the farm now, and he must support his new family."

"Just wait until fall," Mama pleaded.

Carl looked at his parents. He loved them very much. It was going to be a tough decision, but he knew what he had to do.

"I must go to Texas. It is the only answer."

"You're just fifteen," Mama said in a shaky voice.

Papa put his arms around Carl's shoulders. "The boy works like a man now. He must make decisions like a man. We can't be selfish and insist that he stay in Sweden."

Carl's deep blue eyes were fixed on Papa. Carl tried to speak, but no sounds came from his throat. He gripped his father's hand. Words were not necessary to express the bond between father and son.

Carl was both sad and excited. The thought of starting over in a new land with new challenges and opportunities overwhelmed him. Still, he knew he would miss his family. That night he wrote his brother a letter:

Dear Oscar,

I want to come to Texas. I work now in a spool factory but want to be a farmer like you. Please write and let me know if you can pay the passage. I will pay you back as soon as I can.

Carl

CHAPTER 2

Walpurgis Night,
A Swedish Celebration

"Any mail today?" Carl asked his sister each evening, hoping to hear from his brother in Texas.

"No" was her usual reply.

"You're so quiet, *Bror*, you never talk anymore," Christina said. "Is your job at the factory so bad?"

"No, it's the long winter. I go to work before the sun comes up and walk home in the dark. I never see daylight."

He had no future, he thought. His life seemed like the darkness of winter. How he longed for spring.

In early April, the snow began to melt. Carl welcomed the mushy ground that kept his boots always muddy. He smiled as he saw the ice crack on the pond. The days became longer with more sunlight.

With warmer weather coming, Carl thought of Walpurgis Night, the Swedish celebration that welcomed spring. At the end of April, he'd join others in his village to celebrate the event with a bonfire and a festival. He was looking forward to the event.

One evening just before supper, Carl went into his room and sat down on his bed. He glanced at the empty bed where Oscar slept before he left home. Would he ever hear from Oscar? He took his violin from its case and touched the smoothness of the wood. He played a few measures on the instrument, and while still playing he walked into the living room.

Christina heard him playing a Swedish folksong and joined Carl in the living room. She listened intently, her eyes filled with sadness.

"You'll play your accordion on Walpurgis Night, won't you?" Carl asked.

"I have no interest in it this year," she replied.

Carl remembered that a year had passed since her boyfriend, Henning, had left for America. "Last year you enjoyed the celebration," he said gently.

"Yes, but Henning was here," she replied with a sigh.

"I'll play my fiddle if you'll play your accordion. We'll make it a special occasion."

Mama and Papa, hearing the music, came in from another room. Papa looked at his children and rubbed his chin. Carl knew Papa had something important to say.

"I just heard that Sven Anderson from Texas will celebrate Walpurgis Night here with us."

"Will he talk about Texas?" Carl asked eagerly.

"I suppose he will," Papa said impatiently, turning his face away from the family.

"What a wonderful celebration we'll have! Christina and I will play our instruments. There will be a lot of good music to celebrate the end of winter," Carl said.

"Why is this year's holiday so special?" Mama asked.

Carl didn't answer, but the look in his eyes told Mama that he dreamed of going to Texas, and if he left Sweden, this would be his last Walpurgis Night. She turned her head so he couldn't see her face.

"Just play your fiddle," she said quietly.

Carl put his fiddle under his chin and began to play, "Now It's Green Again," the song of spring. He loved playing the old instrument that had belonged to his Uncle Olaf.

"That sounds so pretty," Mama said. "You have a good ear for music."

"I take after Uncle Olaf," Carl replied with a smile.

For weeks before Walpurgis, the men and boys in the village gathered timber from the woods for the bonfire. They piled it in the shape of a giant tepee.

When the night finally arrived, Carl joined the other villagers in feasting, singing, and dancing. He noticed that even Christina smiled as she played, *Sköna Maj Välkommen.* When he wasn't playing his fiddle, Carl led the singing of old folk tunes .

He stopped as soon as he saw Pastor Bergquist stand and raise his hand. "We're happy to have our old friend, Sven Anderson from Texas with us tonight. He'll light our bonfire and speak to us now," Pastor Bergquist announced.

A tall man stood up and held a flaming torch to the pile of wood. As the fire began to blaze, the crowd chanted *"Hurra, hurra, hurra."*

As the flames lit up the sky, everyone cheered. Mr. Anderson adjusted his tie and straightened his coat. Knowing his future might depend on the man's words, Carl listened to every word.

"I am happy to be back in my homeland. You are my *kompis*. I keep you always in my heart. Your friends and relatives in Texas send their love and regards. They are growing large crops in the rich soil of Texas.

"But Texas needs workers. It does not have enough men to plant and harvest cotton and corn. Many farmers will pay passage to America for anyone who will work for them for a year."

"Sounds like slavery to me," one man called out.

"No, it is not slavery. You will be treated well. You will be fed and housed. At the end of the year, you will be free to go anywhere or do anything you wish."

Carl's attention remained fixed on Mr. Anderson. He wanted to know everything about Texas.

"Women are also needed," Mr. Anderson continued. "Wealthy families want Swedish housemaids to work in their

11

fine homes. Again, some families will pay passage to Texas in exchange for a year's work."

Carl looked at Christina, who was listening intently. *Would there be some way his sister could get to Texas?* Carl wondered.

"Texas also needs blacksmiths, carpenters, and other craftsmen. It's a great opportunity," Mr. Anderson added.

Carl visualized warm, sunny days with tall crops growing in the black soil. When Mr. Anderson finished his speech, some of the crowd threw their hats in the air and shouted, *"Hurra, hurra, hurra!"*

More singing followed, and the bonfire burned, sending flames high into the sky. Later, Carl followed the crowd to the *smörgåsbord*. He took a sausage to roast over the fire along with rye bread, cheese, herring, and lingonberries.

He also took a handful of *pepparkaka*. They were his favorite. He ate quickly, hoping to speak with Mr. Anderson before the evening ended. A short while later, he approached the man from Texas.

"I am Carl Olsson. My brother, Oscar, lives in Texas."

"Yes, I know him well." Mr. Anderson replied. "He sends his greetings. He has a wife and child now. His farm produces a lot of cotton But he cannot do all the work. He wants you to come to Texas. He will help you get there."

"I have no money," Carl said, staring at the ground.

"He gave me money to buy your ticket if you will come."

"Buy my ticket all the way to Texas?" Carl asked, astonished.

Mr. Anderson smiled and nodded. "All the way to Texas. He wants you to come as soon as you can."

"I must talk to Mama and Papa about this first."

"Of course," Mr. Anderson said. "I understand. I'll come to your house tomorrow, and we'll discuss this with your parents."

After the festival ended, Carl skipped all the way home. He could hardly wait to talk to Mr. Anderson again. Christina, too, might be able to go to Texas.

Before the man arrived the next day, he spoke to his sister about such a possibility. "Ask Mr. Anderson if you could work as a housemaid in Texas," he told her.

Christina's eyes brightened, then a look of doubt crossed her face. "I don't want to be disappointed. I'll wait and see what Mr. Anderson thinks," she said.

"He seems like an honest man," Carl commented.

As promised, Mr. Anderson arrived the next evening to talk to Carl and his parents. He wore an expensive, dark suit with a diamond stickpin in his tie. Carl had heard the man was a millionaire.

"Texas is a land of challenge." Mr. Anderson explained. "I went there as a young man of twenty. I worked hard and began buying farmland and raising cotton in Fort Bend County. Later, I moved to Central Texas and bought more land and a mercantile store."

Carl hung on the man's every word. *What a story! What a land was this Texas!* he thought.

"I helped many of my fellow Swedes come to Texas, and, in turn, they worked on my farms. You see, I was against slavery, but I needed help on my farms. So I began to pay passage to Texas in exchange for one year of work. I had a very difficult time during the Civil War. I fled to Mexico. But now all that has passed. Do you really think you want to go to Texas?" he said, looking at Carl.

"*Ja,* but I must stay until the end of May and help Papa with planting," Carl replied. "I could leave after Midsommer if Mama and Papa approve."

"That sounds like a good plan," Mr. Anderson said. "What do you think, Mr. and Mrs. Olsson?"

Papa looked at the man's fine clothes, the glittering diamond in his tie. Then he looked at his own worn clothing and his family's modest home. How could he stand in the way of his son's success?

"I want the best for my son. I hate for him to leave Sweden, but if he must, he must."

Carl's face beamed with happiness. His father loved

him enough to let him leave, knowing that he might not see his son again.

"Would there be a chance for me to go to America?" Christina quietly asked.

"Of course. In fact, I know a family that is looking for a housemaid," Mr. Anderson said. "You would be perfect for them. Their home is in Austin, not far from Brushy, where Oscar lives."

As Mama heard the man's words, she dropped the cup of coffee she was pouring. Christina, bending down to pick up the broken pieces, put her arm around her mother. A tear rolled down Mrs. Olsson's cheek.

"I want my daughter to be with good people. Will the family treat her properly?" Mama asked in a choked voice.

"Yes, I would trust the family with my own daughter," Mr. Anderson replied. "But it is your decision, Christina. If you decide to come, you can leave with Carl in late June."

Carl saw the shocked look on his mother's face. "We'll talk about it later," he said gently.

"I will leave so you can discuss this. It's an important decision," Mr. Anderson said. "Just remember that you will not be alone in America. We Swedes stick together and help each other. A man in New York City named Lundblad even meets many Swedish immigrants as they arrive."

"I could lose two children at once," Mama said, her face pale, her lips pursed.

Christina took her mother's hand and patted it. "I should be near Henning. We are engaged. I may not have another chance to go to Texas."

"I know, I know," Mama said, wiping her eyes with her apron.

Papa put his strong arms around his daughter, then his son. Carl rarely saw his father show his feelings. He usually kept them inside, carefully hidden. But on this day he looked at his children with love and sadness in his eyes.

"I want you to know that I will miss you every day of my life," he said.

Axelina, who had been hiding behind a chair, tugged at Carl's trousers. "Why is Mama crying?" she asked.

"Christina and I must leave home," Carl explained.

"You'll be back, won't you?" the child asked.

Carl looked at Mama and Papa, then at Christina.

"Will you be back?" Mama asked.

"I don't know," Carl replied quietly.

CHAPTER 3

Goodbye Sweden

Carl's spirits soared during the following week. He had more energy, walked faster, and talked more. Even his job at the factory seemed less boring. Mr. Anderson, the man from Texas, left two tickets, one for him and one for Christina.

As the days became longer with more daylight, Carl helped his father and brother on the farm. On weekends, he worked for neighboring farmers to earn as much as possible for his trip to America.

When he looked at his father's farm, he noticed that the potato plants were smaller than usual. *There would not be enough food for two families,* he thought. It was good that he and Christina were leaving.

In the evenings, he watched Christina knit, her nimble fingers moving the needles quickly. "What will you do with all those shawls?" he asked.

"I hope to sell them at Midsommer festival. I have no money to take to America," she told him.

"Midsommer, the day the sun never sets, is my favorite holiday," Carl said cheerfully.

"The sun hardly ever sets now. I can knit until long after midnight without the oil lamp," she replied.

16

"In two weeks, we'll be celebrating two occasions, Midsommer and our trip to America," Carl said.

"*Ja*, it will not be long before we say goodbye to almost everyone we know."

"But Henning will be in Texas," Carl reminded her.

She smiled. "I know. Mama, Papa, and Axelina are waiting for us in the kitchen," she added.

Carl saw a pitcher of milk and bowl of potatoes on the table as he sat down. "It is all we have," Mama said.

"Milk and potatoes are nutritious," Christina reassured them.

Carl watched as his father ate very little. He waited until his children had eaten, then he finished what was left. *There would be more food for the family when he and Christina left,* Carl thought sadly.

Later Carl looked out his bedroom window and saw hundreds of pine and fir trees, standing like long statues against the sky. He would miss the trees and the lakes of Sweden.

He lay on his narrow bed and dreamed of Texas and his new life. Then he looked at the bedspread Mama had made him after Oscar left. He closed his eyes tightly and hoped he had made the right decision to leave his home and family.

The days passed quickly and Midsommer had arrived.

"Help me cut some purple laurel from the trees," Christina asked Carl the day before the festival.

Brother and sister walked into the meadow gathering the colorful flowers and the evergreen branches of small trees.

"I think we have enough," Carl stated, looking at the stack of flowers near their house.

"We have to decorate the wagon, too. Don't forget," his sister reminded him.

They picked more wildflowers, placing them over the door of the house along with sprigs of green. Everyone in the village tried to outdo each other in decorating for the festival. The entire village looked like a painting, with splashes of color on every home and wagon.

On Midsommer afternoon the people gathered in the center of the village. Pelle (Carl and Christina's eldest brother) along with three other strong men, held up the Maypole. They carried the cross-shaped pole decorated with bright flowers high above their heads. Christina and two other young women played folksongs on their accordions as everyone marched behind the Maypole.

The old and young danced and sang throughout the evening. Even Papa, who was usually serious, joined in the celebration. Later, families spread picnic lunches on the ground and ate traditional Swedish food: cheese, bread, sausage, and lingonberries.

Finally the villagers walked back to their homes, tired but happy. Only Carl and Pelle remained, reluctant to see the festival end. Carl wondered if he'd ever see his brother again. The two brothers walked slowly home, savoring perhaps the last time they would have together.

At the fork in the road which led to each one's house, they stopped. Carl held out his hand to his brother. "It's time to say goodbye. I'll miss you and the family."

"I'm sorry the farm couldn't provide for all of us," Pelle said, a note of sadness in his voice.

"That is how it is in Sweden," Carl said, shrugging.

"Sometimes I wish . . ." Pelle stopped speaking as if he couldn't find the words. "Sometimes I wish I had the freedom you have, to travel to a new land with new opportunities."

Carl stared at his brother in surprise. He never thought Pelle might want a chance to go to America. The brothers hugged each other for a brief moment, then parted, each going his separate way.

Carl fell asleep as soon as he got in bed. He was still sleeping soundly when his mother's voice awakened him.

"It's time to get up," she said softly.

He sat up with a start, wondering how it could already be morning. Then he remembered what an important day this was, maybe the most important day of his life. He brushed his thick blonde hair from his face, then he dressed for the journey.

In the kitchen, Carl ate *limpa* with white cheese. "Take a loaf with you and some cheese," Mama said.

"I will, Mama. We'll enjoy the bread for as long as it lasts. After that, we'll make do with whatever the cook on the ship serves us."

The Olsson family was quiet at breakfast. Only Axelina broke the silence. "Will you give me a pony ride if I come to Texas?" she asked.

"*Ja,*" Carl replied, hoisting his little sister on his shoulders and running around the room as if he were a pony. Mama, Papa, and Christina laughed while Axelina collapsed in giggles.

Carl dreaded saying goodbye. He began to put the trunks of clothing on the wagon waiting in front of the house. As he walked back, Papa handed him a black case.

"Take the fiddle," Papa said.

"But it belonged to Uncle Olaf," Carl protested.

"You're the only one who can play it. I'll feel better knowing you're taking something from Sweden with you to that distant land."

Carl hugged his father, then his mother and little sister. He knew it was time to leave. He waited for Christina at the wagon and saw that Mama put something around her neck. Christina then hurried to join Carl.

As Christina stepped into the wagon, Carl noticed that she wore a gold locket around her neck. "It belonged to *Mormor,*" she said with a sob in her voice.

"I'm glad you have it. And I have Uncle Olaf's fiddle," he said, touching the old case lovingly.

"Well," the driver said as they climbed onto the wagon. He waited until Carl took a coin from his pocket.

"Payment to take us to Forserum," Carl said.

As the horses pulled the wagon away, Carl heard his father shout in a loud voice, "God be with you."

Carl touched his sister's shoulder gently to remind her that he would be with her, sharing the adventure. Traveling over the Swedish countryside, Carl gazed at the lake, sparkling like gems between the groves of trees. "Sweden, the land of lakes. How I'll miss this," he whispered.

He reached in his pocket, took out a crumpled piece of paper and showed it to Christina. "This map shows where we are going. First we catch a train at Forserum and go to Göteborg. Then we travel by ship to Hull, England. Then to Liverpool by train and finally by steamer to America."

"It's a long trip," Christina said thoughtfully. "But we're together, at least."

When they arrived at Göteborg, Carl looked up at the Swedish flag and said, "We must leave our country and our family."

Christina stared up at the blue and gold flag. "I know, Carl. We say goodbye to Sweden. Our adventure begins here."

Brother and sister boarded the steamer headed for Hull, England. They stayed on the top deck, enjoying the cool, brisk wind that blew from the North Sea.

Thoughts about the future passed through Carl's mind. Christina looked at him with fear of the unknown in her eyes.

"What kind of place do you think Texas is?" she asked.

"I think it will be a wonderful place for those who aren't afraid; those who don't mind adventure."

"I'm trying to picture Oscar's farm. I wonder how it looks and what cotton is like," she said. "It will be so different for us. But I'm glad we're going. Do you think that Henning will be glad to see me?"

"Of course he will. He'd be a fool if he wasn't."

A smile came over Christina's face as she looked at the sea. The hours passed quickly. When they arrived in Hull, England, Carl looked at the pleasant, clean town.

"Such a beautiful place," he said. I wish we could stay awhile, but we must hurry to the train station."

The two left the steamer, pulling their luggage behind them. Just as they arrived at the station, Carl heard the conductor call, "Liverpool, all out for Liverpool." They rushed aboard.

When the train arrived in the large city of Liverpool, Carl and Christina saw a town covered with soot and dirt from factory smoke. Their eyes burned as they walked the streets.

"Don't look, Christina," Carl said as they passed poor, ragged children begging.

"I wish I could help them," she said.

"Me too, but we have little money for ourselves. We must spend a night here, but we'll leave early in the morning," Carl told his sister.

The immigrant hotel where the travelers stayed was dirty and crowded. Carl took out the remaining bread and cheese that his mother had given them. They ate in silence.

In the morning, they walked to the dock where a large steamer awaited them. Carl looked at the whale of a ship, painted gray and black. He had never seen such a ship. The name, S.S. *Hero,* stood out in bold letters on the side of the ship.

"The ship is run by steam," Carl told his sister. "But see the sails above. In case the motor fails, the sails will keep us going."

Several Englishmen going to America joined them on the ship. Carl nodded to them since he spoke no English. Then brother and sister walked the gangplank to the upper deck, their luggage trailing behind. The captain dressed in dark blue uniform addressed the group of Swedish immigrants first.

"Ahoy, mates, we'll be almost 2,000 people on board, along with cargo we're taking to America. Welcome one and all. Your mattresses are over there," he said in Swedish, pointing to a pile of thin, used mattresses.

"We have to sleep on those?" Christina asked, wrinkling her nose.

Carl nodded, then walked to get his mattress. Christina followed hesitantly.

"Swedes and Englishmen below. The Irish will join you soon on your voyage to America," a sailor announced.

"We're steerage class since we paid less money. That's why we go way below deck," Carl explained to his sister.

"Women at one end, men at the other," another sailor shouted.

"I'll see you at meals," Carl told Christina, as they separated.

Later that evening they met for supper in the dark, crowded area. "What kind of food is this?" Carl asked, frowning at a gray, greasy mixture.

"It's soup and be thankful for it," Christina said.

The sun shone brightly the next two days, and the Atlantic Ocean was calm as a bayou. The immigrants talked among themselves. Sometimes they sang. Carl played folksongs on his fiddle while the Swedes and Irish hummed the tunes. He always kept a careful eye on his fiddle, taking it with him when he left his bunk.

Carl was grateful for the peaceful voyage. He had heard of other voyages that were rough and stormy. Unfortunately, the good weather only lasted two days. On the third night Carl was awakened by a crack of thunder and the sound of waves slapping the sides of the ship. The vessel rocked from side to side, and when Carl tried to stand, he was knocked down by the motion.

Dizzy and nauseated, Carl lay back on his bed. He grabbed a can and vomited everything he'd eaten. Other immigrants also suffered from sea sickness. Carl held his head as the ship's rocking and foul odor made him sicker. He longed for his family and wondered if he'd ever see Texas. He felt as if he might die.

Finally, toward morning, the sea calmed, and the ship stopped rocking. Carl no longer heard waves lashing against the sides of the ship. When he sat up, the dizziness was almost gone. Gradually, the nausea disappeared.

Carl got up and washed his face in the small amount of water that was given to him. His body ached as if he'd been very ill, and he had a headache. His face was pale as a cloud. He wondered if Christina had also been sick.

He walked to the ladies' quarters and saw Christina sitting very still. There were dark circles under her blue eyes. "I feel awful. I'm sure I will die," she said.

"It is a terrible sickness, I know. But you won't die. You'll feel better soon," Carl assured her.

"I wish I'd never left Barkeryd," she cried.

Carl looked at his sister, wondering how he could help her. Nothing but time would help, he knew. She lay back on her mattress, not wanting to speak anymore.

On the upper deck, Carl inhaled the fresh sea air. The wind blew in his face, and he felt normal again. But when he returned below deck, the same sour smell greeted him. He gagged, trying not to vomit.

Would anything be worth this discomfort and loneliness? he wondered. He left the steerage again for the upper deck. A torn map of the United States lying nearby caught his eye. He picked it up, scanning the outline of the eastern part of the country. He wondered how much longer the trip would take.

Nine days later the captain announced, "We are approaching your new country."

CHAPTER 4

Castle Garden, the Immigration Center

"Look, Christina, I see tall buildings. This must be New York City," Carl said, jumping up and down.

As he stood on the upper deck, he saw an American flag blowing in the wind. He took off his cap to show respect to the Stars and Stripes.

Christina took her brother's arm, then squinted to make out the outline of the city. "We're really here, *Bror*!" she exclaimed.

The captain appeared on deck and gazed into the faces of immigrants from many lands, who were waiting to begin new lives. "We dock at Castle Garden, the Immigration Center," he announced.

Carl looked at the tongue-shaped piece of land. "Castle Garden," he commented as he looked at the red, sandstone building.

A sign on the fence surrounding the building read, "Nation's Gateway." Carl looked at the sign written in English and knew the foreign words meant that he and immigrants like him must enter the United States at this point.

"You will be examined by doctors to determine if

you're healthy, free of disease, and have your smallpox vaccination papers. If you have no criminal record, you can then enter the United States," a man explained in Swedish.

Carl began to perspire, worrying if he'd be allowed to enter the country. His heavy clothes stuck to his body as the hot sun beamed overhead. What experiences lay ahead of him? Would this really be the land of opportunity? He and Christina slowly walked across the gangplank to Castle Garden.

The old building, dirty and in need of repair, bulged with immigrants from many countries. Steaming-hot bodies pressed against each other like sardines. Many immigrants, tired and hungry, fell asleep on the floor. The smell of dirt and unwashed bodies filled the building.

Carl sniffed and frowned. After weeks of living below deck, he still was not yet free to enter the new land.

"This doesn't look like a garden to me," he remarked.

"I know. But I heard that plays and concerts were performed here in the past. Jenny Lind, the famous Swedish singer, even sang here," Christina replied.

"It must have looked different then. I don't know if I can stand this for three days or not."

Sailors unloaded the immigrants' trunks from the ship. Carl still wore his violin around his neck. He didn't trust these strangers who stole from each other.

Carl and Christina slept on their coats on the floor that night, using knapsacks for pillows. They both prayed that morning would come soon.

The people sleeping around them woke up early the next day. Bowls of porridge, a thick, lumpy gray mixture, were passed around to Carl and the others. He looked at it with distaste, but he was too hungry not to eat it.

"I hope I'm healthy enough for these Americans," he told his sister. "I think our time for examination is near."

Carl followed the men in one room, while Christina went with the women into another room. "Where are your vaccination papers?" an examiner asked Carl.

Carl looked at the man blankly. He could not understand what the man had said.

The immigrant next to him who knew both Swedish and English translated the question. Carl reached in his pocket and handed the vaccination paper from Sweden.

An American doctor then listened to Carl's heart and lungs. He checked Carl's skin and body for signs of disease, then mumbled, "Pass."

Carl, assuming he could leave, walked quickly into the larger room to wait for Christina. Soon she walked up to him, a smile on her face. "I passed," she said.

The small group from Sweden remained together, feeling some comfort in being able to speak the same language.

The next morning a sailor approached them. "You are free to leave," he said. "One of our guides will walk you to the city and give you directions."

Pulling their trunks on ropes behind them, Carl, Christina, and the others walked across the drawbridge. They looked like typical immigrants in their "Old World" clothing. The men's long coats were of heavy wool, and their caps almost covered their faces. Christina's dress came to her knees, and her bonnet was dark and plain. The unsettled looks on their faces revealed who they were: strangers in a strange land, uncertain but hopeful.

Carl noticed many types of boats along East River — barges, ferries, steamships, sailing ships. Tall, narrow smokestacks, like black trees, rose from the vessels.

The guide pointed in one direction. "Broadway is that way. It is the widest street in New York City and maybe the whole country," he said proudly. "You can walk down Broadway to the end and return the same way. You won't get lost if you stay on Broadway."

"Where is the immigrant hotel for Swedish people? Mr. Lundblad arranged for us to stay there," Carl told the guide, remembering Mr. Anderson's words.

"Three blocks to the right, then two to the left," the guide replied.

Carl and Christina smiled, relieved. But before they began the walk, they looked up at the skyline of the city. "The buildings must be six stories high." Christina said, wide-eyed.

Along with the other Swedish immigrants, they walked to the hotel. Located in a narrow building, a small sign said, "Lundblad Hotel."

Carl entered and looked around. "We need a room for tonight," he said with uncertainty.

The Swedish-speaking clerk nodded and motioned for them to follow him down a narrow hall. Carl and Christina walked into a small room with two twin beds.

"It will do," Carl said, looking at the plain room.

They walked to the washrooms in the hall, one for men and one for women. Carl washed his face and felt refreshed. Then he realized he hadn't eaten since breakfast. He was ravenously hungry.

On the street outside he saw pushcarts filled with everything from flowers to fish. He stopped at one and asked for *mjolk*. The man stared at him curiously, then pointed to a jar of milk. Carl took the milk, along with some cheese and a hunk of bread. He gave the man an American dollar that he had exchanged from Swedish money on the ship. The pushcart owner took the money and handed Carl some change.

Carl smiled and nodded in thanks. "Finally, I can have some good, sweet milk. I have not tasted any in many days."

They sat on a park bench and ate their food. "The cheese is different from our white Swedish cheese, but it is still good," Christina said.

Much later at the hotel, Carl sat down on one of the beds and said, "This feels like a board, but I can sleep anywhere tonight."

Christina felt the locket around her neck, making sure her grandmother's necklace was still there. Then she fell asleep.

The voices of other immigrants awakened Carl and Christina the next morning. They rose, dressed, and walked into the tiny lobby. The clerk handed them a handwritten note from Mr. Lundblad. It said: "I will come for you in my carriage this morning and take you on a sightseeing tour. We will have lunch in my home."

Christina's face brightened. "We will not have to be alone in the city, after all."

Outside the hotel they saw a handsome carriage drawn by white horses. The driver stopped and a man inside came out. "*Välkommen,* I am Vilhelm Lundblad. I hope you had a pleasant journey. I'm sorry I could not meet you at the harbor yesterday. But I had important business to attend to."

"We were able to find the hotel," Carl reassured the man. He looked at Mr. Lundblad, dressed in a tailored, dark suit with a cravat at the neck. Was he another Swede who had made his fortune in America?

"I want to show you Central Park and other beautiful parts of our city," Mr. Lundblad said.

They drove down Broadway first, and Carl remembered that it was the widest street in New York City. He looked at the fine buildings many housing jewelry and clothing stores. His eyes rested on wealthy Americans who wore tall top hats and carried canes. Most of the women had fine bonnets with matching parasols.

"This is Central Park," Mr. Lundblad said. "I hear a band playing. We will sit on the grass and listen."

Red, yellow, and orange flowers bloomed in the gardens. Carl and Christina sat on soft, green grass under the shade of elm trees.

"Band music," Christina said in an excited voice.

They watched and listened as musicians in uniforms played rousing band tunes. The conductor wearing a blue-plumed hat directed the rhythmic tune, his arms moving with precision.

"They're playing the 'Washington Post March' by John Philip Sousa," Mr. Lundblad said. "He is a great American composer."

"Such fine American music!" Carl exclaimed.

"*Ja,* I like the rhythm," Christina added, tapping her foot to the music.

When the band stopped playing, Carl heard people

speaking many languages. He understood why America was called the "melting pot" of the world with its many races and people from every country in the world.

After the concert ended, Carl and Christina joined Mr. Lundblad in the carriage. They rode through much of New York City before arriving at Mr. Lundblad's brownstone home.

"My driver will take the carriage. Please come in for a cup of tea. Then we'll have lunch."

Carl stared at the brownstone that was located in a fashionable section of New York City. He had never seen such a fine place.

Inside, they sat in the parlor. A servant served tea and small cakes on a silver platter. Carl and Christina drank the good tea from china cups.

Mr. Lundblad, a tall, silver-haired man with a gentle voice, seemed eager to talk with his visitors.

"I want to know about my homeland, my Sweden," he said.

"Little rain has fallen in four years. Times are bad and food is scarce," Carl replied solemnly.

"I am truly sorry. But tell me about some good times, too. Tell me about Midsommer."

Carl and Christina took turns describing the recent Midsommer festival in their village. Carl remembered each detail of his last day in Sweden. As he spoke, Mr. Lundblad listened with a faraway look in his eyes.

"Such a beautiful country, Sweden. It is sad that people cannot earn a living. It's so different from America. Of course, not everyone is rich. But it is easier to earn a living. Sven Anderson says you are going to Texas."

"*Ja,* our brother lives there," Carl explained confidently.

"I owned many acres in Texas at one time. I had large cotton farms. My uncle and I were in business together. Now I'm a banker here in New York."

Carl listened carefully to the man's words. He knew that this new land was full of opportunity.

They ate lunch later in the day in a large dining room. Carl stared at the table full of good food.

"Ah, herring, it has been a long time since I tasted it," he told Mr. Lundblad.

"Enjoy your lunch, dear boy," the man said. "You have a long journey ahead of you tomorrow."

"We will travel by steamer to Galveston, Texas," Carl informed him.

"I have already sent word to my friend there, Pastor Fosberg. He will meet you. You see, we Swedes want to help you newcomers to the United States."

"Thank you," said Carl. "My brother will also help. He will teach me to farm cotton."

"Texas is a good place to live, but quite different from Sweden. You will miss the lakes of your homeland," the man said.

After lunch, Mr. Lundblad drove with his chauffeur to take Carl and Christina to the hotel. They arrived just before dark.

"God be with you," Mr. Lundblad said as he left them.

Carl remembered that his father had said those very words the day they left Sweden.

CHAPTER 5

Welcome to Texas!

Mr. Lundblad's chauffeur took Carl and Christina to the harbor the next morning to board a steamer bound for Texas. It was a smaller ship, and the hull was painted sea-blue.

"We will be at sea four days," the captain announced. "We deliver cargo in Florida before we arrive in Galveston."

"This is our last trip on water," Carl said. "I'll be glad to keep my feet on solid ground."

When he saw what they would be having for dinner that evening, his good mood changed. "Boiled potatoes and rye crackers with molasses on them is all we get?" he complained. "We'll starve before we get to Texas."

"You can endure a little more discomfort. Be patient awhile longer," Christina said in her big-sister voice.

Carl lay awake that night, listening to his stomach rumble. He tried not to think of food for the next two days as he ate the small amount he was given.

Early on the fourth day at sea, he and Christina were on the upper deck breathing the fresh air. He touched his sister's arm, and said, "I think I see land in the distance."

A short while later, the captain appeared on deck. "We are nearing Galveston Island," he said.

"I told you!" Carl cried out.

Seagulls dove at the ship, looking for morsels of food. Fluffy, white clouds floated above the blue-green Gulf of Mexico. Fish jumped as the ship churned through the water, making foamy waves.

"I can't wait to put my feet on Texas soil!" Carl exclaimed.

"We survived, *Bror*, we're in Texas," Christina said with a sigh of relief.

The ship docked in Galveston Harbor a short while later. Carl and Christina showed their identification papers to the officials and received permission to enter the island. They trudged along the gangplank, the last one they had to cross. The trip to Texas had ended.

"Mr. Lundblad assured us that Pastor Fosberg should be here." Carl commented, looking around for a friendly face.

The pair stood squinting in the Texas sun, their wooden trunks behind them. Carl still wore his violin around his neck.

Soon a man with a round, rosy face approached them. "*Välkommen.* You must be the Olssons. I am Pastor Fosberg."

The man smiled broadly and shook their hands. "I will drive you to my home, which is not far away."

The horses pulled the wagon down a brick street to a small, white house. Mrs. Fosberg, a short, plump woman with graying hair, greeted them at the door.

"Come in and be comfortable. I have good, sweet milk and ginger cookies for you," she said, smiling.

Carl eyed the platter of cookies that looked just like the ones his mother made in Sweden. *What a treat,* he thought.

He and Christina quickly drank the milk and devoured the cookies. *"Tack så mycket,"* they told Mrs. Fosberg.

Carl looked out the window and saw the beach, its sand glistening in the sunlight. "Could we walk to the beach?" he asked. "We've never seen sand like that."

"It's very hot now," Pastor Fosberg warned. "Better to wait until later."

"We won't stay long. I have to touch the sand and see it up close," Carl replied.

The man shrugged. "Just don't stay too long."

Carl and Christina walked two blocks and sat down on the warm sand. "It looks almost like snow," Christina said.

"*Ja,* but it's hot," Carl replied.

He let the crystals flow through his fingers, marveling at the feeling. "I'm taking off my shoes, rolling up my pants, and wading in the water," he announced.

Christina lifted her long skirt and joined her brother as the wet sand oozed between their toes.

"I found a star-shaped shell," Carl said.

The pair walked on the beach, enjoying the sun and the sand. When they looked behind them, they realized they had been walking a long time.

"Your face is red as a flame," Christina said.

Touching his hand to his face, Carl exclaimed, "I feel like I have a fever!"

They walked back to the house, and Mrs. Fosberg took one look at them, shook her head, and said "You two look like boiled crabs." Here, use the juice from this aloe plant. It will help ease the burning."

Carl and Christina squeezed the sticky juice on their skin. Gradually, the pain lessened. Then Carl smelled food and realized he hadn't eaten since breakfast.

"I'm a good Swedish cook," Mrs. Fosberg said. "You can eat as much as you can hold."

When they sat down at the simple table, Carl thought of his mother in Sweden. He felt as if he were back in her kitchen.

They ate white cheese, chicken, brown bread and of course, potatoes. They also drank plenty of milk.

"I made an *ostkaka* for dessert," the woman said.

"I can't believe it!" Christina exclaimed. "I never thought I'd taste it again."

After eating the rich, cheesy custard, Carl and Christina

complemented Mrs. Fosberg's cooking. Pleased, she showed them the room they'd share that night.

"I'll drive you to the train in the morning," Pastor Fosberg said. "The train leaves early. You have a long day's journey ahead of you."

The next morning Carl and Christina told the Fosbergs goodbye. Carl was grateful for the pleasant visit. Mr. Anderson was right; the Swedish people help each other in the new land. He waved as the train left for Central Texas.

"Ah, Sister, the miracle is just beginning. We're starting our new life in Texas," Carl said happily as the train chugged through the countryside. He wanted to chat with his sister, but the noise of the engine made it difficult.

As the hot air blew in the window, Carl loosened his collar and took off his coat. Christina pushed up her sleeves, trying to stay cool.

"The land is so flat," Carl remarked. "There are trees, like in Sweden. But there are no lakes that I can see."

At that moment, the train crossed a narrow bridge over the Brazos River. The old engine shimmied and shook, and Christina clutched the arm of her seat.

"We might drown in the river before we even see Oscar," she said.

After traveling for several hours, Carl stood up and stretched his legs, feeling the heat and fatigue. "There isn't a cool breeze here like there was in Galveston," he said.

"My mouth is full of dust," Christina said. "I wish we had a drink of water."

The train ride lasted all day. Late in the afternoon, the conductor announced, "All out for Brushy."

"We're here," Carl said joyfully. "We survived the trip."

"Where is Oscar?" she asked, concerned.

"He'll be here soon. I'll unload our trunks."

They went inside the station to wait and escape the brutal afternoon heat. The clerk gave them cups of water to quench their thirst.

"I'll look for Oscar again," Carl said after a few minutes.

Outside in the heat he looked around. He scratched his

neck. The heavy wool shirt he was wearing itched. His hair was moist under his wool cap. The local men, mostly farmers, stared at Carl and smiled.

Did he look so different from them? he wondered. He glanced at his wool pants and heavy snow boots from Sweden. In contrast, the Americans wore blue overalls made of a lighter fabric.

As he gazed beyond the depot, he spotted a wagon drawn by two strange-looking animals. They resembled horses but had long, floppy ears. He strained his eyes to see the driver of the wagon, who he hoped was Oscar. But the driver was not Oscar, so he gave up and went back inside the depot.

As Carl entered the depot, he saw Christina wipe the dampness from her face, wisps of hair limply falling across her forehead. The clerk looked at them curiously. He was counting money as if he intended to close for the night. Carl longed to speak to the clerk but he knew no English. He wanted to tell the man why they were waiting and ask how long they could wait.

"No sign of Oscar," he told his sister.

"I think the depot is closing. We'll have to wait outside."

The clerk shook his head sympathetically as the pair dragged their trunks to a covered porch area outside. Even though the sun was sinking, the air was still hot. Carl looked in all directions, hoping to see his brother. After a short while, a wagon approached the station.

Carl stared at the face of the driver; it was the color of walnut, not at all like Oscar's face. But the man seemed to be looking for someone. He stared at Carl curiously, his straw hat tilted back slightly. Then a smile came over his face.

"Carl, is it really you?" he cried out in Swedish.

Was this dark-skinned, thin man Oscar, the husky brother who left Sweden four years before? Why had he changed so much?

"*Ja,* I am Carl, but I hardly recognized you."

"The hot Texas sun turns the body darker. But, you,

Carl, you're taller than I am. You were just a *pojke* when I left Sweden," he said, patting Carl on the back.

Then he turned to Christina and kissed her cheek. "My dear sister, you're prettier than ever."

"Older, too, and still not married," she said with a wink.

"There will be time for that later."

After piling the trunks in the back, the three of them climbed into the wagon. Carl put his violin on his knees.

"What are these strange animals that pull the wagon?" Carl asked.

"Mules," Oscar replied. "Half-donkey, half-horse. They are very strong animals for plowing. I don't have any oxen."

"Is your farm near?" Christina asked, as they traveled down a dirt road.

"*Ja,* half an hour. We'll be there before dark. You'll like my wife Ingrid. She comes from Stockholm in Sweden. My little boy Erik is three years old."

Carl and Christina told about their journey from Sweden and the discomforts they'd endured. In a short while, Oscar turned into a narrow road leading to his house. Carl could hardly see because it had grown dark, but he did observe that the roof was slanted just like his house in Sweden.

A tall woman with long blonde braids met them at the door.

"*Välkommen,*" she said, smiling warmly and taking their hands. "We're so glad you're here."

Carl liked her at once. He liked her eagerness and sincerity. Little Erik, a child with wheat-colored hair that fell over his forehead, eyed his new aunt and uncle curiously.

"Please, sit down," Ingrid urged, as they entered the house. "Our chairs are sturdy but hard. Oscar builds our furniture. We don't have fine things."

"This is the living-room and bedroom in one," Oscar said. "Our house is small. You will share this room. Ingrid, Erik, and I sleep in the other bedroom."

"I like the room fine," Christina said. "I wish I could stay longer, but I must travel to Austin to work."

"I wish you didn't have to leave Brushy. I've been looking forward to having a sister-in-law. Austin is so far away. It's about twenty-five miles from here," Ingrid commented.

"I know, but I must work for the family who helped me come to Texas. I'll move to Brushy after I've repaid them," Christina explained.

Carl sensed that his sister was eager to ask about Henning. Finally she asked. "Have you seen Henning?"

"*Ja*, he works nearby. We are so busy that we see him only at church on Sundays. We told him you were coming today," Oscar said.

Carl saw the disappointment in his sister's eyes. He knew she expected Henning to meet her at the depot. She looked away, and Ingrid put her arm around her.

"Let's have supper. I know you two are hungry. We eat a simple meal at night — bread, butter, sweet milk, and cheese," she told them.

Carl ate heartily. His stomach was empty after a day without food. Oscar was eager to talk about Sweden and their family.

"How are Mama, Papa, and the others?" Oscar asked.

"They are sad that the family must be separated, but they want the best for all of us," Carl told him.

"Texas is a good place to live. You'll like it. Of course, it's different from Sweden," Oscar explained.

Carl's head began to nod and his eyelids grew heavy as Oscar talked on. Finally, Ingrid came to the rescue.

"Carl and Christina need rest. Tomorrow will be another big day." Then turning to her guests, she said, "The privy is behind the house. The washbowl is in the kitchen."

Carl slept on a pallet on the floor that night, while Christina slept on a mattress stuffed with cotton. Tired from the long journey, they both fell asleep immediately.

CHAPTER 6

The Cotton Fields

Early the next morning, Carl and Christina were awakened by little Erik.

"*God morgon,*" Carl said, ruffling Erik's hair.

The little boy grinned and pulled at Carl's sleeve. He led his uncle and aunt into the kitchen where Ingrid was cooking a big breakfast on her wood stove. Carl stared at the platter of eggs, sausage, brown bread, and butter.

"Ah, *limpa,*" he exclaimed, his mouth watering. He smeared a piece with rich, creamy butter.

Oscar passed the plate of sausage. "We don't have much money, but we have plenty of food. Eat up. Then I'll show you my farm."

Christina enjoyed her breakfast, although she ate much more slowly than Carl. Eager to see his brother's farm, Carl ate quickly, but he savored each mouthful.

A short while later, Oscar led his brother through the barnyard. Chickens clucked and scattered as they walked past. At the back of the barnyard, hogs grunted and wallowed in the dirt.

"Here are my two cows. They give us all the milk,

cheese, and butter we can eat. We even sell some to the store," Oscar said. "And my good old mules, Olle and Stig, pull my plow."

As they walked even farther, Carl saw a green field with plants as tall as his knees. "So this is cotton," Carl remarked. "This Texas is a miracle land. I feel like I'm in heaven."

He touched a white blossom, feeling the softness of the cotton.

"Cotton bolls," Oscar said, grinning. "When they finish ripening, we'll pick them and take them to the cotton gin. That's how I earn money."

"A lot of money?" Carl asked.

"It depends on how many bales of cotton I get to the acre. This year's crop looks good."

Carl picked up a handful of the black soil, smelled it and smiled. "Such good soil, so different from Sweden's."

"*Ja,* a man can do well in Texas. Land sells for about four dollars an acre. I'm saving to buy more. Not everybody is as wealthy as Mr. Anderson, but we make a good living."

"Where is Mr. Anderson? Will we see him?" Carl asked. "I'd like to thank him for helping us."

"He's moved to West Texas, where he owns a large ranch. He will visit us sometime, though. He likes to help other Swedes come to America."

"I hope I can be as successful as you are," Carl told his brother.

"You will." said Oscar. "You're young and energetic. Now let's walk back to the house and get a drink of water from my well."

They stopped at the well near the house. A round, stone wall surrounding it reminded Carl of the wells in Sweden. Oscar lowered a bucket on a rope into the well and brought it up with water. "Here, drink," he told Carl, handing him a tin cup.

Carl tasted the cool water, then gulped it down. They stood for a moment, looking at the cotton farm. Carl marveled that such a crop could grow so well. He also saw the stalks of corn drying, to be used for animal food later.

As he looked past the farm and down the road, Carl spied a man walking. "I think it's Henning," he said. "I must tell Christina."

Carl rushed in the house. "Henning is coming!" he shouted.

Christina's eyes brightened. She brushed back the strands of honey-colored hair from her face and pinched her cheeks to make them rosy.

"Come in," Carl said, shaking Henning's hand. "It's good to see you again."

At first, Christina seemed shy in front of the tall man in overalls. But he embraced her eagerly, planting a kiss on her cheek.

"You're very pretty, just like I remembered. It's been over a year since we saw each other," he said.

She nodded. "You look good, too, but your skin is darker."

"The Texas sun turns even a pale Swede's skin brown. But you won't have to worry. You'll be working inside."

"*Ja*, I've been blessed. It's a miracle I'm even in Texas. I'm grateful to Mr. Anderson for finding someone to pay my passage."

"We all have much to be thankful for. I've almost paid back the money for my ticket to Texas. But I have to work and save money to buy a few acres," Henning said.

A short while later, Henning left for work but returned that evening for supper. After they ate, Carl helped Ingrid clean the kitchen so that Christina and Henning could take a walk. He was pleased to see his sister looking so happy.

Two days later Christina's train ticket to Austin arrived just as Henning came to visit. Carl heard his sister tell her boyfriend that she must leave soon.

"Please write me," she said in a low voice.

"I promise. I hope the Littleton family will let you visit us in Brushy. If not, I'll find a way to come to Austin," Henning replied.

"Please do. A train ticket costs $1.30, which is more than I can afford."

The next morning Carl hitched the mules to the wagon and drove his sister to the train station. He wanted to tell her that he'd miss her, but he couldn't find the words. She had given him strength and courage on the long journey.

"We've had many hardships, Christina. But our dream is starting to come true."

She nodded. "I'm a little scared, though. I hope the family is kind."

"Mr. Anderson assured us they are fine people." As he hugged his sister, Carl felt a tear on her cheek.

He watched the train until it was out of sight. He wished the best for his sister. When he got back to the house, Oscar was waiting for him.

"She will be taken care of," Oscar said in a kind voice.

Carl helped with the farm animals that day. He fixed a harness on the mules, slopped the hogs, and fed the chickens.

That evening Oscar told him about the work ahead of them. "We need to chop weeds between the cotton plants. I'll wake you early so that we can start work by daylight. You can wear some of my old clothes. Your old woolies will be too hot."

When his brother shook him awake the next morning, Carl was snoring softly. "Get up, *Bror*, we work while it's still cool."

As Carl staggered into the kitchen, he saw a table filled with fried eggs, biscuits, and cheese. He helped himself to generous portions of everything, taking big mouthfuls of eggs and biscuits. He chewed fast, swallowed, and crammed his mouth full again. He saw Ingrid looking at him with a smile on her face. He realized he'd already eaten twice as much as Oscar. Embarrassed, he put his fork down.

"My table manners are not so good. I keep thinking I'm in Sweden, and I won't see this much food again."

"I understand," Ingrid said. "I remember how difficult it was in those days."

She was quiet for a moment, then she said, "At noon I cook a big meal that we call dinner. At night we eat a light supper of bread and cheese."

42

Carl drank the last sip of his milk, then followed Oscar outside. "Here, wear this straw hat," Oscar said. "So you won't have a sunstroke."

They walked past the barnyard, then came to the cotton field. Carl looked up at the cloudless sky with a smile on his face. Such a land, Texas, he thought, gazing at the tall plants. It was a farmer's dream.

The hot sun soon convinced him that life in Texas was not perfect. Carl had not sweated so much in his life. That night his face was tomato-red. The skin felt tight, as if it had been stretched over the bones of his face.

"Here," Ingrid said, handing him an Aloe vera plant. "Squeeze the juice on your face to help the burning."

"Mrs. Fosberg in Galveston gave us this for sunburn," Carl said, doing as his sister-in-law advised.

The following days Carl worked beside his brother, weeding the field. Once he looked up to see a small dark cloud coming his way. He ducked, fearful that a swarm of bees would sting him. He ran in the other direction, but the black cloud followed him.

"Come back," Oscar called. "It's just a swarm of grasshoppers. They're leaving."

"Do they harm people?" Carl asked.

"No, but they can eat a crop in a few hours. Be glad they're gone."

"Texas is a place where the sun burns your skin and insects destroy crops in a short time. Sweden doesn't have these nuisances," said Carl.

"No, but we couldn't raise crops like these in Sweden, either," Oscar said.

Carl nodded, knowing his brother was right. Even though he was hot and tired, Carl continued chopping weeds, a boring but necessary job. As he chopped, his mind wandered to Sweden and thoughts of his family. *How were Mama and Papa? How was the potato crop there?* he wondered.

Then a strange, buzzing sound brought him back to the present. *Was the sound coming from a bird or animal?* he wondered.

Looking more closely, Carl saw a dark coil resembling a rope on the ground. Then a head emerged.

"I see something strange," he said to Oscar, who stood about six feet away.

"It's a snake, Carl. Don't move."

The buzzing sounded again. Carl's feet seemed to be glued to the ground.

"The snake has diamonds on its back," Carl said softly.

"It's a rattlesnake, Carl, and it's poisonous. You must chop it with your hoe."

Carl's legs felt like jelly. His arms hung limply at his side. Fear, like an arrow, pierced his body.

"Take good aim and chop the snake," Oscar urged.

Could he do this? Carl wondered. Several seconds passed and the buzzing began again. Carl lifted the hoe high above his head and brought it down with all his strength.

The snake wiggled and slithered on the ground. *Had he missed it?* Carl worried. If he had, the snake might strike him; it might kill him. He stepped back, sweat dripping in his eyes.

Oscar moved closer, looking at the ground. "You got the mean devil. You killed him. Snakes wiggle even after they die. You did what you had to do, Carl."

Carl moistened his lips with his tongue. He breathed heavily as he watched the snake finally stop moving.

"We've had enough excitement for the morning. Let's go back to the house," Oscar suggested.

They stopped at the well near the house and Carl took deep drinks of cool water from the tin cup. After he quenched his thirst, he stood under the chinaberry tree, trying to forget the frightening experience.

Later, as Oscar and Carl told Ingrid the snake story, her eyes widened and she shook her head. "You must be more careful," she warned Carl.

Carl nodded. "*Ja.* No more rattlesnakes for awhile."

CHAPTER 7

A Visit to the Bergmans

"We go to church on Sundays," Ingrid told Carl a few days later. "The service is in Swedish so you'll understand."

"I have only my hot Swedish coat to wear," Carl said.

"You don't need to wear a coat. Men don't in summer," she explained. "And you can borrow a cotton shirt from Oscar."

"*Tack så mycket,*" Carl said, thinking Ingrid was almost like a sister.

Carl squeezed into Oscar's shirt. He was glad he had something cool to wear. Oscar drove them to church in his wagon.

Inside the church, Carl observed how simple it was — certainly not as fine as his church in Sweden. People sat on crude, wooden benches. A few plain windows, not stained-glass ones, let in a little light.

"Follow me," Oscar directed. "The men sit on one side of the church and the women on the other."

Carl sat down beside his brother on the hard bench. As the first hymn began, "How Great Thou Art," Carl thought of Sweden, his home, and his parents. They often sang the same hymn at his old church.

He enjoyed hearing Swedish spoken by others besides just Oscar and Ingrid. As he left the church after the service, a boy his age walked up to him.

"Are you from Sweden?" the boy asked.

"*Ja,* I am Carl Olsson."

"I'm Gusten Bergman. My mama and papa came from Sweden but my sister and I were born here. We speak English and Swedish. Will you come visit us sometime and tell us about Sweden?"

"I'd like to very much," Carl replied with a smile.

Carl watched the dark-haired Swedish boy meet his parents at their wagon. Perhaps he'd have a friend his own age soon.

The ride back to the farm took only a short while, and Carl played with Erik while Ingrid cooked the big Sunday dinner. He was impressed by the feast she'd prepared. He took a large helping of potatoes, his favorite. As he tasted the vegetable, though, he frowned, wondering why it was so bitter. He tried to spit it out but didn't want to be rude. He managed to swallow the mouthful.

Oscar watched, then began to laugh. "That's a turnip, *Bror,* not a potato. We grow lots of turnips here. You'll learn to like them."

Carl nodded but doubted he'd ever like the taste of turnips.

"Oscar played a trick on you," Ingrid said, while giving her husband a scolding look. "So I have a special treat for dessert, peach pie from the peaches on our trees."

Carl looked at the strange fruit lying in rich pie crust. He'd never seen peaches before. Ingrid poured fresh cream over his helping. As Carl took a bite, juice trickled down his chin.

"Dirty," Erik said, pointing his finger at Carl.

Carl wiped his chin on his sleeve. "*Ja,* I must be more careful. This pie is juicy."

After Sunday dinner, Ingrid, Oscar, and Erik rested in their room. Carl was glad to have some time alone. His life was so different now. He wondered about Mama, Papa, and

Axelina. How he longed to see them. How he longed to see the lakes of Sweden. He decided to write a letter to his family:

Dear Mama, Papa, and Axelina:

We had many adventures on our trip to Texas, some good and some bad. Christina and I arrived safely and well. She works in Austin, 25 miles away. Papa, I wish you could see Oscar's cotton farm and this rich soil. I miss you and wish I could bring this good earth to Sweden. Then we could grow all the food we need there. You can not imagine how hot the weather is in Texas.

Your son,
Carl

Carl put down his pen and closed his eyes, imagining he was back in Sweden. He could almost hear little Axelina's laughter and smell Mama's bread baking.

The next week Carl worked side by side with Oscar in the cotton field. In addition, he helped care for the hogs and mules and did any other chores that needed to be done. He still wondered about Christina and if her employer was kind to her.

One day as he fed the mules, an American farmer stopped and spoke to Oscar. Oscar turned to Carl, explaining that the farmer wanted Carl to work for him on Saturday.

"I won't need you that day if you want to work for him," Oscar told him.

Carl nodded yes, thinking of the chance to earn money. His small amount of savings was almost gone, and he was still working to pay Oscar for the ticket to Texas.

When the weekend came, the American neighbor came for Carl in his wagon. At the farm the man gave Carl a hoe to weed the cotton. Carl worked steadily in the hot sun, sweat pouring down his face and back.

At noon the farmer motioned for Carl to sit under a big oak tree. His wife brought Carl a plate of stew and cornbread. The man said something in English to his wife and smiled. She nodded and grinned. They then left Carl to eat his meal alone. He labored all day and earned fifty cents.

Later, at home, Carl turned to Oscar, a curious look on his face. "What does the American mean when he says 'dumb'?"

Oscar hesitated, then a troubled look came over his face. "Did the American say 'dumb' to you?"

"*Ja,* he said 'dumb Swede.' "

"One meaning of dumb is 'stupid,' " Oscar explained.

"But I am not stupid," Carl protested, his face reddening.

"I know that. Dumb can also mean unable to speak. That is what the American had in mind. You did not speak to him."

"I couldn't speak to him because I don't know English."

"I understand. But some Americans call us 'dumb' just because we are silent and don't talk."

Carl stared at his brother, his lips clamped shut. He cracked his knuckles in anger. He had never felt inferior to others. How could he trust these Americans who called him cruel names?

"*Bror,* the Americans aren't cruel to us. They just don't understand us." Oscar explained. "You have to learn to ignore some things."

"I wish I could study English. I don't want to be a *främmande* forever."

"You have no time for that now. You'll learn enough English to survive, just as I have."

Carl started to speak, to tell Oscar what was in his heart. But he didn't want to argue with his brother, who had helped him come to Texas. But why couldn't Oscar see the importance of learning English?

On Sunday, Carl looked forward to going to church and hearing Swedish spoken. He hoped to speak to Gusten again and know him better. Finally, Sunday came and they went to the small church.

Before the sermon began, a handsome woman almost as tall as Carl, rose from the pew. She began to speak:

"I want to invite all Swedish immigrants to attend the free English classes at the church. We supply books and help you with pronunciation. Please come on Wednesday afternoon."

Carl's blue eyes lit up like sapphires as the woman spoke. He thought she was speaking directly to him. As he walked out after the service, she caught his eye.

"I know you're new in Texas," she said in Swedish.

Carl nodded. "I am Carl Olsson."

"And I am Inga Lindell. I hope you can join us on Wednesdays. It's so important to learn the language of the people here."

"I want to, but my brother needs me on the farm."

"Oh," she exclaimed, obviously disappointed. "Maybe you can come later. You'll always be welcome."

Carl smiled at the slender woman, her thick blonde hair piled high on her head. *"Tack så mycket,"* he said.

He knew she would be a good teacher. She could teach him to speak like the Americans. Deep in thought, he didn't realize a girl was speaking to him.

"I know you're Carl. I'm Lisa Bergman. I like the way you sing," a girl said, her flaxen hair trailing to her shoulders.

"Was I singing too loud?" he asked, his cheeks turning pink.

The girl smiled. "No, I didn't mean that. You have a good voice. I am Gusten's sister. I want you to meet my parents."

On the steps outside she turned to an older, pleasant-looking couple. "Mama, Papa, this is Carl Olsson."

"Ah, I understand you're from southern Sweden," Mr. Bergman said.

"Ja, from Småland."

Carl shook hands with the Bergmans, who seemed happy to meet someone who just arrived from their homeland.

"We have not returned to *Sverige,* since we left eighteen years ago," Mrs. Bergman said sadly.

At that moment Gusten joined them. "Could Carl have Sunday dinner with us?" he asked.

"Of course," Mr. Bergman said.

Oscar and Ingrid, standing nearby, heard the conversation. As Carl started to ask their permission, his brother nodded and smiled. *"Ja,* visit the Bergmans."

Carl grinned with gratitude, then followed the Bergmans to their wagon. In just a few minutes, they arrived at a large white farmhouse. It looked twice as big as Oscar's and had white, lace curtains on the windows. Such a fine place, he thought. He dreamed of having a house like this.

They ate the noon meal at a large dining room table. Carl noticed a bowl of chicken and gravy with biscuits floating on top.

"Those are dumplings," Mrs. Bergman explained, passing the bowl to Carl.

He ate the tasty dumplings, savoring the rich chicken gravy and tender meat. He watched Gusten bite into an ear of corn. He had never seen such a vegetable in Sweden. Carl bit into his corn too deeply, getting a mouthful of cob. Gusten, who watched him from the corner of his eye, laughed out loud. Carl blushed.

"You can spit it out. You bit too deep," Gusten said.

Embarrassed by his ignorance, Carl tried again to do as Gusten did. *Maybe he was a dumb Swede, after all,* he thought.

"Do you like Texas?" Lisa asked, changing the subject.

"*Ja,* a good place. But so different from Sweden and so hot," Carl answered.

"A strong boy like you can work hard and save your money. You'll be able to buy land in a few years," Mr. Bergman said. "Gusten, you should follow Carl's example."

"All this talk about work makes me tired," Gusten said, grinning. "Isn't it time for dessert?"

Mrs. Bergman nodded to Lisa, who went to the kitchen and brought in a large pie. "It's blackberry pie from the blackberries we pick in the field," she explained.

Carl stared at the red-black pie oozing with juice. As he took a bite, he liked the tart taste. The berries were not as good as the lingonberries of Sweden, but they were still tasty.

"The dinner was delicious," he told Mrs. Bergman. "Food is so plentiful in Texas."

"We raise chickens, hogs, and some cattle. Our cows give us fresh milk, cheese, and butter. And our garden provides us with vegetables all year. My wife cans beans and tomatoes," Mr. Bergman said.

"My parents would be shocked at so much food," Carl commented.

Gusten fidgeted a bit, then nudged Carl. "I think we've finished our meal. May we leave the table? I want to show Carl my horse."

The Bergmans nodded their consent. On their way to the corral, Gusten turned to Carl. "Do you ride?"

"A horse?"

Gusten laughed. "I didn't mean a cow!"

Carl shook his head. "I've never been on a horse."

A few minutes later Gusten patted the neck of a black and white horse. "This is Smokey. We have another we call Ripper, but he's too wild to ride yet."

Gusten put the bridle over Smokey's head, threw a blanket over her back, then a saddle. "Watch me first," he told Carl.

"Giddap," he said loudly and loosened the reins. Smokey trotted out to the corral and then around it. Gusten brought her back to Carl. He dismounted the horse, and led her to Carl, who stood back.

"She's O.K. You can ride her. I'll show you how," Gusten said.

"Put your left foot in the stirrup while holding the reins. Then swing your right foot over her back and put it in the other stirrup. Make sure you grab the saddlehorn. When you're ready for her to go, loosen the reins and yell 'Giddap.' "

Carl, though unsure of himself, did as Gusten instructed. He held the reins tightly at first, and the horse walked around the corral. Feeling more confident, he loosened the reins and said, "Giddap."

The horse left the corral and trotted into the pasture. Carl's head bobbed up and down in the wind as the horse picked up speed.

"Pull in the reins," Gusten shouted.

Carl didn't hear his friend and gaining confidence, he began to enjoy the ride. He rode on, unaware of the distance. When he saw Gusten running toward him, he shouted "Whoa," and pulled the reins. The horse came to an abrupt stop, giving Carl a jolt.

"Not bad for a beginner," Gusten said, out of breath. "Now get off the horse as you got on, from the left."

As he dismounted awkwardly, Carl's feet touched solid ground, and he felt relieved. "She's a great horse," he said. "You're very lucky to have a horse of your own."

"I'd rather ride a horse than do anything, especially study and go to school."

Carl looked at his friend with envy.

"Do you study arithmetic?" Carl asked.

"Sure, and all those other boring subjects. You know, history, grammar. You're lucky you don't have to go to school."

"I don't feel lucky. I wish I could learn new things. I want to read books in English. But I probably won't ever be able to go to school again."

"You might someday," Gusten said sympathetically.

The boys walked back to the house, and Carl told the Bergmans goodbye. "Come see us again," Mr. Bergman said.

Lisa smiled shyly at Carl as she said goodbye. He felt lucky to have such good people as the Bergmans for friends.

He walked home slowly, passing fields of tall cotton plants growing in neat rows. The white bolls or blossoms seemed almost ready to burst. Arriving at his brother's farm, he saw Oscar standing outside.

"Did you enjoy your visit with the Bergmans?" he asked.

"*Ja,* they were very kind to me."

"The boy Gusten is a wild sort." Oscar warned. "Don't see him often."

"He is the only friend I have."

Oscar shrugged and went inside.

"Mrs. Lindell spoke of English classes at church," Carl said, following his brother into the house.

"I heard. But I told you, Carl, that there isn't time for studying English now. You work for me, and you must do as I say."

Oscar just would not understand, and Carl knew that he had to obey his brother. Carl tried to control his anger.

He went outside and sat under his favorite tree. Taking out a pocket knife, Carl whittled on a piece of wood. He scraped the wood vigorously, trying to rid himself of his anger. He knew if he could speak English, he wouldn't be called "dumb" again. He wanted to talk with Christina; she'd understand. But she was twenty-five miles away.

Several days later, almost as if she'd read his mind, Carl received a letter from his sister:

> Dear Ingrid and Brothers,
>
> My employers are very kind to me. I keep house and cook for a family of five. Mrs. Littleton bought me new clothes and is teaching me some English. I hope you're learning the language, too, Carl. I hope the cotton crop is doing well. Please drop me a line.
>
> Lovingly,
> Christina

Carl reread his sister's letter, happy she was content and treated kindly. How lucky she was to learn English.

CHAPTER 8

Picking Cotton

The next day Carl helped Ingrid pick green beans and tomatoes. He had never tasted tomatoes and wasn't sure he liked them. But since they grew in the garden and Ingrid served them at every meal, he knew he had to try them.

"I'll can beans today," Ingrid said. "They'll taste good this winter when the fresh vegetables are gone."

Later that afternoon, Carl helped his sister-in-law screw lids on the hot jars. Ingrid's face turned as red as the tomatoes she canned and sweat dripped from her neck and arms. The kitchen seemed like a blazing furnace to Carl.

After they finished canning, Oscar walked in the kitchen, a solemn look on his face. "I don't like the looks of those clouds. It could rain any day and ruin the cotton crop. That would mean six months of hard work and no money to show for it."

"Should we start picking tomorrow?" Carl asked eagerly.

"*Ja,* we start at sunup. Come, help me finish storing the corn in the barn before dark."

After finishing that chore, Carl washed up and ate supper with his brother and sister-in-law. He went to bed early that night, thinking of the day ahead. He always liked harvest in Sweden when the crops were ripe and ready for picking. Picking cotton in Texas would be a new adventure.

Oscar awakened Carl before daybreak the next morning. They ate fried eggs and biscuits hurriedly before going to the field. As the sun rose, Oscar handed his brother a long cloth sack to hang around his neck.

"For the cotton," he explained. "Pull the bolls from the top. Try not to get much stem with it."

As the morning passed, the cool air turned hot, and the sun beamed down on Carl's neck. His straw hat shielded his head from the sun, but his body dripped with sweat. At ten a.m., after five hours of work, the brothers sat under a tree to rest. Oscar brought water for them to drink.

"Is that all you've picked?" Oscar asked sharply.

"*Ja*, I picked as fast as I could."

"You're too slow. We'll never be finished."

Not wanting to disappoint his brother, Carl tried to pick faster. He realized that his dream of success in America would require more work than he thought.

At noon, Carl welcomed a break. He and Oscar returned to the house to eat Ingrid's dinner of chicken and vegetables. After resting, they returned to the field.

By the end of the day, Carl was exhausted. His arms and shoulders ached. Dirt and sweat made a beaded circle around his neck.

Near the water well, Oscar pointed to a round tub, about thirty-six inches in diameter. "We bathe here," he said. "You can fill the tub with the pail."

Carl filled pail after pail with water, pouring it into the wooden tub. Finally, he stripped, hanging his clothes on a bush. As he stepped into the tub, the cold well water chilled his body, but he felt refreshed. His dirty clothes would dry, and Carl would wear them again. He didn't have enough to change every day.

Ingrid washed clothes once a week. It was an all-day job. Carl helped by filling a washpot with water over an outdoor fire. Ingrid would drop in bits of homemade soap, then use a scrubboard to get the stubborn dirt from the clothes. When the pot was emptied, she added clean water for rinsing. After squeezing water from the clothes, Ingrid hung them on the fence to dry. Her hands were rough and red.

For the next several days, Carl and Oscar rose at dawn to pick cotton. They worked nine hours a day, going to bed at dusk.

Oscar was in high spirits, encouraged by the picking. "We may get a bale of cotton per acre," he said. "You can go to the cotton gin with me soon."

"What happens at the cotton gin?" Carl asked, puzzled.

"Machinery sucks up cotton from the wagon, then pulls the cotton fiber from the seed. The cotton is packed into bales and the seed is left in the sack," Oscar explained.

Carl could hardly wait to make the trip to the gin. Oscar promised that they would also go to town and to the store.

"Buy a good piece of cloth at the store, and I'll make you a Sunday shirt," Ingrid told him.

On Saturday the brothers dressed in clean clothes and started off with the heavy wagon load of cotton.

They went to the cotton gin first. It was a noisy, busy place. The sound of machinery was deafening, but Carl enjoyed the excitement. Wagon after wagon was lined up loaded with cotton, waiting to be unloaded. This was the end of many months of hard work for the farmers.

Carl noticed as he walked through the line of wagons that the American farmers stared at him curiously. Was he so different from them? Yes, Oscar's overalls were too short for him. And his boots from Sweden were old-fashioned. His hair looked as if it had been cut with a bowl placed over his head.

Whatever the reason, Carl felt like an outsider, especially when one of the Americans spoke to him, and he couldn't understand. The farmer shook his head in disgust.

"Foreigner," the man yelled. "Why can't you learn English?"

Oscar, busy seeing that his cotton was unloaded, didn't

know who the farmer was talking to. Then he realized the farmer was speaking to Carl.

"He's only been here a month," Oscar explained.

The farmer grumbled and went about his business.

Oscar turned his attention back to the man in charge of unloading. The man spoke to him, and wrote in his notebook.

Oscar's face brightened as he turned to Carl. "Almost two bales to the acre!" he exclaimed.

He jumped up and down. Then, after gaining control of his emotions, he handed Carl a sack. "Here, I saved some cotton seeds. We'll plant them next spring. Come on, get in the wagon, we're going to the store."

"Giddap," Oscar yelled to the mules.

"You will get much money?" Carl asked.

"*Ja,* not today, but soon." His usual solemn face beamed with pleasure.

Carl's anticipation grew as they rode into downtown Georgetown. He eagerly awaited seeing the center of the business community.

"This is the courthouse, which is an important building," Oscar said as they rode down the main street. "All records of land ownership, births, marriages, and deaths are stored here. It is also where judges hold trials for people accused of crimes."

"Like horse thieves?" Carl asked.

Oscar nodded, then brought the wagon to a halt. Carl noticed different storefronts that formed a square around the courthouse.

"An apothecary, a saddlemaker, a blacksmith shop, and a barber shop," Oscar explained, pointing to the stores.

He tied the mules to a hitching post in front of the mercantile store.

"I almost forgot," Oscar added, reaching for a sack. "Here is the lunch that Ingrid packed for us."

Carl ate quickly, eager to see the main store in town. When they walked down the aisles of the store a few minutes later, Carl stared at the items in amazement. Never had he seen so many different objects for sale in one place. He saw tools of all kinds, workclothes, and barrels filled with dried beans, flour, sugar, salt, and coffee beans. His eyes lingered on a pair of shiny cowboy boots. How he longed for a pair.

Oscar picked up a fifty-pound sack of flour and twenty pounds of sugar and put them on the counter. He added a large sack of coffee beans and box of salt.

Carl stared in disbelief at the number of items Oscar selected. He hoped his brother would have enough money. He almost forgot to choose a piece of white cloth for his shirt. But at the last minute, he found a piece.

"How much?" he asked Oscar, holding the cloth.

"It costs ten cents. I'll pay for it. You've been working hard."

Carl looked at his brother in surprise.

Oscar carefully counted the money he owed, making sure he had enough. Finally, he grabbed a handful of peppermints for Ingrid. "She loves sweets," he explained to the owner.

"Thanks for the business," the man said. "Is he your brother?" he asked, looking to Carl.

"Yes. Name is Carl. From Sweden," Oscar said in broken English.

"Welcome to Texas, Carl," the man said, shaking his hand.

Carl beamed with pleasure at the man's friendliness. Not all Americans were alike, he thought.

Walking out the store, they passed long, wooden boxes. "What are those?" Carl asked.

"Coffins for dead people," Oscar replied laughing. "We shouldn't need those for a long time."

They arrived at the farm just before dark. It had been a long day, but Carl felt elated. He watched Ingrid's face break into a big smile when Oscar handed her the candy.

"Did you get the white cloth?" she asked.

"*Ja*, it's here," Carl said, handing her the cloth.

"Good, I'll make you a new shirt."

Carl's face flushed with pleasure. What a day this had been. He wished every day would go so well.

Oscar's happiness over his crop continued all week. They went to church on Sunday, and Carl saw Gusten after the service.

"Come to the farm, and I'll give you another riding lesson," Gusten told him.

With Oscar in such a good mood, Carl decided to visit his friend right after Sunday dinner. Gusten was riding his horse as Carl walked up.

"I'm glad you came," he said.

He dismounted the horse and motioned for Carl to take over the reins. Carl felt much more confident this time and enjoyed riding through the pasture and back again.

"You're doing better," he told Carl. "You can be a cowboy like me one of these days."

"Someday I'll have my own horse," Carl said confidently.

"You shouldn't have to wait forever. People sell horses all the time. On the first Monday of each month Georgetown has a cattle and horse sale. We'll go to it sometime."

Carl's eyes had a dreamy look. Would he really own a horse of his own? He could imagine riding with Gusten over the countryside, exploring, seeing new things. He knew it was a dream, but sometimes dreams come true.

"Have you ever been in a cave?" Gusten asked suddenly.

Carl didn't reply. He was still thinking about the horse he planned to own someday.

"I know of a cave on the west side of Georgetown. Some people say there's hidden gold there. Want to go with me to see it?" Gusten asked.

"Gold in a cave? *Ja*, we go."

Carl visualized sacks of gold nuggets waiting for them to discover. If he found gold, he could do many things. He could bring his parents to America, buy a horse, cowboy boots, even a farm.

"I'm ready to go if you have the nerve," Gusten said.

"Let's go now," Carl agreed.

CHAPTER 9

The Search for Gold

The boys mounted Gusten's horse and started down the road. "The cave is on the west side, the rocky side. Only cactus and a few cedar trees grow there," Gusten told Carl.

"Why do you think there's gold in the cave?"

"Long ago the Spaniards came here with sacks of gold and silver from Mexico. They buried it in a cave for safe-keeping. They planned to return for it but never did."

Carl listened carefully and imagined huge sacks bulging with treasures. "Has anybody seen the gold?"

"I don't know for sure. People won't talk about what they've seen. They don't want others to know about it."

"Do you really think we'll see gold?"

"We might. But it's dark and scary in the cave. Are you brave enough to go with me?" Gusten asked.

Carl didn't answer as the boys rode through the rugged countryside. They stopped in a rocky area that reminded Carl of Sweden. Gusten tied his horse to a fence post.

Gusten led the way through cactus and cedar trees, then up a rocky hillside. Walking down the opposite side of the hill, they looked down.

"There it is," Gusten said excitedly.

As they descended the slope, Carl spotted a limestone bluff. Gusten pointed to an opening at the bottom.

"We can enter here," Gusten said.

Carl saw that the opening was only three feet high. "We have to crawl through there?" he asked.

Gusten laughed. "Yes, but it's not as small as it looks."

"How can you find gold in the dark?" Carl asked.

"With this lantern. It gives a lot of light. You want to go in first?"

"No, you go first," Carl replied.

"Promise you'll follow me?" Gusten asked.

Carl thought a minute. He didn't want to go in the cave. But he knew he must. Gusten would think he was a coward if he didn't.

"I promise," Carl answered.

Gusten ducked his head and crawled in the cave, then he motioned for Carl to follow. Carl slid in behind his friend. The light from the lantern made him feel safer.

Carl observed every crevice around him. The wider tunnel led to other openings. Cone-shaped rock formations hung from the ceiling. He shivered in the cold, damp air.

Gusten walked a few steps, then stumbled.

"The bottom is wet and slippery, watch out," he warned Carl.

"Have you seen deeper parts of the cave and tunnels?" Carl asked.

"No," Gusten confessed.

Carl guessed that his friend had never been in the cave before.

"Want to explore in there?" Gusten asked, pointing to a narrow tunnel."

"I'm not so sure," Carl said. "I don't like this place."

"We could be the first to find gold," Gusten urged. "Shouldn't we try?"

"Go ahead, I'll follow."

Gusten held the lantern in front of him, leaving Carl in half-darkness. He started to follow, but Gusten told him to wait.

In a matter of minutes, Gusten returned. "I don't think a man could crawl through there, especially carrying gold."

The walls of the cave glistened in the lantern light. Carl felt its strange beauty as he touched the rough, wet walls with his fingers.

Suddenly, fluttering sounds came from the top of the cave. Carl froze in his steps as he heard high-pitched bird-like cheeps. Gusten shone his lantern on the ceiling.

The boys stared in shock at hundreds of small birds hanging by their feet from the top of the cave. Their wide wings covered their tiny bodies like coats.

Carl breathed heavily as he stared at the birds and heard their strange sounds. *Would the birds harm them? Were they dangerous?* he wondered.

"Bats," Gusten said in a low voice. "They won't hurt us. But let's get out of here."

Carl was first to crawl through the cave's opening. The bright sun made him blink.

"We'll bring two lanterns next time," Gusten joked.

Carl shook his head. He doubted if they'd ever return to the cave. As they walked outside, the sun's rays beat down on the boys, a sudden change from the cold cave air. Carl wiped the sweat from his face on his shirtsleeve.

"We need to cool off," Gusten said. "I know a place on the river called Deep Hole. The water's always cold."

The boys rode Gusten's horse to a narrow neck of the river. A steep cliff rose on one side. Gusten tied his horse to a tree, then climbed the cliff. He took off his clothes and jumped in the river. Carl followed him, the cold water chilling him to the bone.

"It's the spring water. We'll stay cool the rest of the day," Gusten promised.

They dove from the cliff again and again, swimming in the cold water. Refreshed, they dressed and rode back to the Bergman farm.

"The sun is sinking," Carl said as they rode. "I need to get back home."

"I want you to see Ripper first, then I'll take you to Oscar's farm."

Carl spied Ripper, a large, sleek horse in the corral. His dark mane blew in the breeze as he pawed the earth, showing off his power.

"I'd love to own a horse like that," Carl said.

"But he's wild. I have to break him."

"Break him? Hurt him?" Carl asked, alarmed.

"No, just teach him who's boss," Gusten replied.

Carl reached out to touch the horse's flowing mane, but the horse reared up, snorting loudly.

"I told you he has a mind of his own," Gusten said.

Carl watched the stallion gallop off, his muscles straining, almost as if he were showing his power. What a strong, fine horse Ripper was.

"It's getting late. I should be going home," Carl said. "I forgot about milking."

"You worry too much about what your brother thinks."

As they rode to Oscar's farm, Carl looked at Gusten and asked, "Do you think I could buy a horse for $15? I don't mean a beautiful one like Ripper, but a nice horse not too old?"

"Sure, if a farmer doesn't want to feed a horse and doesn't need one, he'll sell."

Carl smiled at his friend. "I'll work hard, save every cent I can working for the Americans. If I had a horse of my own, I'd feel really free."

Gusten rode off, and Carl walked up to his brother's house. He saw Oscar in the doorway.

"You missed milking tonight. Were you riding with Gusten again?"

"*Ja*, we hunted for gold in a cave. Maybe we'll find it if we try again."

"Gusten told you that old story of hidden gold? There's no truth in it. Someone would have found the gold by now. You wasted the entire afternoon. Horses and farming don't mix," Oscar continued. "I had to do all the chores tonight. You spent too much time with Gusten."

"He is my only friend."

"You have family. Families are closer than friends," Oscar said sternly.

"I love my family. But I need friends."

"There are other Swedish boys here."

"But they haven't been as friendly to me as Gusten has."

The brothers said no more. The next day Carl worked harder than usual. He wanted to please Oscar. They picked cotton each day, trying to finish the tiring chore. Carl longed to see the end of cotton season.

Gradually Oscar forgot his anger, and Carl felt that his brother had forgiven him. The cotton crop had been successful, and Oscar's pride showed in his face.

"I may buy more land," he confided in Carl. "If I add acres each year, someday I'll own a huge farm."

"*Ja,* that's the way you succeed in America, by working hard. I want to have land of my own someday," Carl said.

"I'll try to pay you wages at the end of the year when you've repaid me for your ticket to Texas."

"I know you'll be fair," Carl said.

"I probably will never be rich as Mr. Anderson. Not many people are that lucky. But if you work hard, you can live well in this state."

As Carl thought about his brother's words, he realized the chances of becoming rich were slim. But he still had his dream, the dream of being a real American and speaking English.

That night he wrote his parents a letter:

Dear Mama and Papa,

I have not heard from you. Please write as I miss you very much. I like Texas, but it is different from Sweden. I cannot speak English to the Americans. I go to the Swedish church and have met one good friend. He has two horses.

Picking cotton is hard work, but Oscar has good crops. I also work extra for the Americans when I can. It is very hot in Texas, nothing like cool Sweden. I wish you good health.

Your son,
Carl

CHAPTER 10

The Cattle Drive

"Our hard work is over," Oscar told Carl a few days later.

The muscles in Carl's neck and arms ached. His face was bronzed by the Texas sun. Each night before bedtime, he used the juice from an aloe plant to soothe his skin.

"Will you go to the gin tomorrow with the last load?" Carl asked.

"No, a cattle drive is coming through town. I don't want to be caught in that cloud of dust."

"What's a cattle drive?" Carl asked.

"Cowboys in America lead hundreds of cows across the country, taking them to market. They travel through many states, including Oklahoma, Kansas, even Colorado."

Carl stared at his brother in disbelief. He couldn't imagine hundreds of cows walking through Georgetown. What a sight to see!

"Since we've finished picking cotton, I'd like to watch the cattle drive tomorrow," Carl said.

"*Ja*, go, but don't get trampled," his brother warned.

"Trampled?" Carl asked. Surely his brother was teasing

him. The thought of cowboys and hundreds of cows wandering through Georgetown made him too excited to sleep.

The next day he walked past the Bergman farm on his way to town and saw Gusten outside. "We had a holiday from school today. Want to ride my horse?" Gusten asked.

"I want to watch the cattle drive. Could we ride your horse to town?"

"Yes, you take the reins. I'll ride behind you."

The boys rode Smokey to the outskirts of Georgetown. They tied the horse to a post, then sat on the wooden fence to await the herd.

"You've never smelled anything so bad as the manure the cows leave on the trail. It really stinks. But watching the cattle drive is worth it," Gusten added.

Shortly, the deafening sounds of 2,000 hooves hitting the earth grabbed Carl's attention. In the distance, he saw cows trampling the earth in a cloud of dust half a mile long.

"The cattle are coming," Gusten shouted.

Townspeople, wagons, and horses scattered as the herd thundered over the main road leading to town. The cattle moved steadily, destroying grass and ignoring other animals, people, and anything else in their path.

Carl saw a cowboy sitting arrow-straight in his saddle, hat pulled over his forehead. His face was walnut-brown, creased with lines made by sun and wind. He and another cowboy rode in front of the herd.

Next came the lead steer, a brown and white animal with wide horns and a large, brass bell around his neck. His hide was scarred and rough from countless trail rides.

"That's a Longhorn steer," Gusten shouted.

Carl stared at the animal, its massive horns chipped from fights with other steers or encounters with trees and cactus. Carl had seen pictures of these animals.

"Longhorns are the toughest of all cattle. They can survive cold weather and hot weather. Then can even survive without food for long periods of time," Gusten told Carl.

Cowboys rode on each side of the herd, keeping the animals together. Dust flew in the boys' eyes and covered their faces as the herd charged through town. The cows let out loud, bellowing sounds as their hooves hit the ground.

"Eee–ahh," a cowboy yelled, riding his horse near the herd to keep it in line.

"Cowboys have to listen for every sound or movement or the cattle could stampede," Gusten said.

Carl watched, his eyes wide with amazement. Never had he seen such huge, tough animals. One wrong act could cause the herd to scatter in many directions.

"The cattle will cross the San Gabriel River soon," Gusten told Carl. "Let's ride to the river and watch."

The boys arrived at the river just as the first cows plunged in the shallow water. The animals drank greedily, pushing each other with their broad shoulders and nudging with their horns.

After getting their fill of the cool water, one group of cows waded across the narrow river to the opposite bank. Carl looked at the muddy river and thought of the clear lakes of Sweden.

As the boys rode back to town, Carl frowned at the damaged trail. The herd had changed the trail into torn and broken ground, a sea of dust. No grass survived the visit of 800 Longhorns.

"My papa says the herd walks fifteen or twenty miles a day. It takes months to get to market. The cowboys work from sunup to sundown. They sleep outdoors. I'd like that kind of life. Someday I may be a cowboy," Gusten said, watching the last of the herd disappear from sight.

"I'm glad it didn't rain today. The town would have been one giant mudpuddle," Gusten added.

The boys rode back to town, and Gusten tied his horse to a hitching post. He stopped to look at a saddle on a horse tied next to his.

"That's a handsome saddle," he said. "It would look good on my horse," Gusten said.

He turned to Carl. "With everyone inside, a person could take that saddle and never be seen."

"You mean steal it?" Carl asked.

"No, just take it for fun. If you'll stand watch, I'll try."

"What if you get caught? Your Papa would beat you."

"I won't get caught." said Gusten. "Come on, Swede. Haven't I been your friend?"

"*Ja*, but I can't steal."

"Just keep watch for a few minutes and tell me if anybody comes out of the store."

"I can't do that," Carl said.

"You're a chicken and dumb Swede at that," Gusten taunted.

"I'm not dumb. Don't ever call me that," Carl said, doubling his fists at Gusten.

"So you want to fight? I'll smash that blonde head of yours and blacken your eyes," Gusten threatened.

Gusten pushed Carl against the store, pinning his shoulders against the wall. Carl kicked Gusten in the chest and knocked him down.

A man came from the store and gave the boys a stern look. "What's going on? No fighting is allowed."

"We're just having an argument," Gusten said, getting up.

As the man walked away, Gusten's face glowed red with anger. "I'm leaving. If you want a ride home, you better get on the horse and make it fast."

On the way to the farm, Gusten made his horse gallop and Carl bounced up and down on the back of the horse. Carl breathed a sigh of relief when they arrived at the Bergman farm.

"I'll get Smokey some water," Gusten said, dismounting.

Carl removed the saddle and brushed the horse's coat without saying a word.

"I still think you're a coward," Gusten said.

"I went into the cave with you," Carl replied, defensively.

"If you want to prove you're brave, ride Ripper."

"But Ripper is still wild," Carl protested.

"I've been working with him. He's better. I can ride him. Don't you have the guts?"

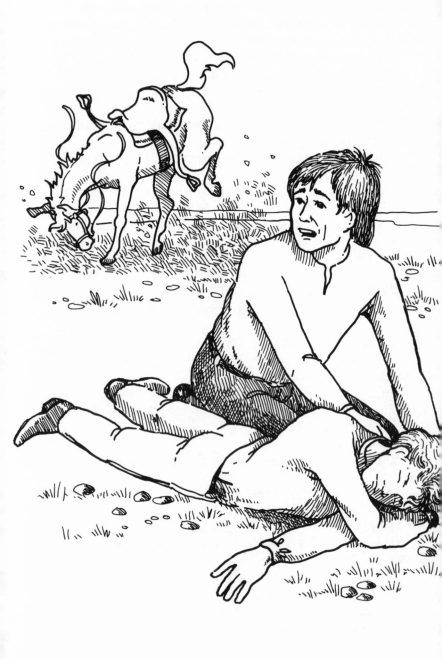

Gusten glared at Carl, waiting for his answer. Carl knew he had to accept the challenge. "I'll do it," he said.

Gusten approached Ripper cautiously, removed the halter and put the bridge around his neck. Ripper balked at the bit in his mouth, shook his head and snorted.

Gusten threw a blanket, then saddle over the horse's back, then tightened the cinch. "Get on," he shouted.

Carl took a deep breath and gritted his teeth, trying to summon the courage to ride the wild horse.

"Don't you have the nerve?"

Determined, Carl put his foot in the stirrup, but Ripper whinnied and pulled away.

"I'll hold the reins. Get hold of the saddle horn as soon as you put your foot in the stirrup."

Carl tried again. He threw his leg over the horse's back. Angry at the pressure, Ripper took off running. A pale, frightened Carl sat wedged in the saddle, his knees close to the horse. Clutching the reins, Carl tried to sit still, but he bounced up and down. Ripper galloped into the pasture, then bucked, his front legs clawing the air. Then Ripper's back legs kicked out as his head dipped low. Carl slid forward, holding on for dear life.

Ripper ran without any direction, then stopped and danced on his hind legs like a rodeo bronco. Carl rose from the saddle and despite his best efforts, fell to the ground. He felt a crack in his leg as he landed. Ripper continued running like a gazelle while Carl lay motionless on the ground.

When he tried to get up, sharp pain shot through his leg. "Something's wrong, Gusten."

"I'll get Papa. He'll know what to do," Gusten said, now worried that his father would discover how he dared Carl to ride the wild horse.

In a few minutes, Mr. Bergman came. He patted Carl's arm gently, his face solemn.

"I'll carry you to the house. We must get the doctor."

"Not a doctor," Carl protested. "I have no money to pay a doctor."

"You may have broken your leg. Only the doctor knows

for sure," Mr. Bergman said. "We'll worry about the money later."

Gusten's face turned pink. He started to tell his father the truth when Mr. Bergman interrupted. "Ride your horse to the doctor's office and ask Dr. Monson to come as soon as he can."

When Gusten returned to the farm, half an hour later, Carl was lying in bed, very still, his face very pale.

"Dr. Monson will come soon," Gusten explained.

"I'm better, I don't need a doctor."

A short while later, Dr. Monson arrived, an older man with long, gray beard. He looked at Carl curiously.

"So you fell from a horse and hurt your leg? You haven't been in Texas long enough to ride horses, young man."

Carl closed his eyes and bit his lip to hide the pain as the doctor examined his leg. Dr. Monson felt Carl's toes, foot, leg, and thigh. Then he shook his head.

"You've fractured your leg. It's not a bad break, but I must put your leg in a splint. The bone must be kept straight and still. You can't move your leg until the bone heals."

"But I won't be able to walk or work on the farm," Carl cried.

"Not for awhile," the doctor replied. "Gusten can make crutches from a tree limb so you can move around."

Carl's face became even paler as the doctor gave instructions to the Bergmans. "I need two flat pieces of wood for the splint. Narrow pieces from a tree trunk will do, Gusten. And Mr. Bergman, please help me put Carl's bone back in place."

"I'll have to hurt you in order to set your leg, Carl. I'm sorry. You can bite on this piece of wood if the pain is too much. Or you can yell," the doctor added.

Carl dug his fingernails into the palms of his hands and looked at the ceiling, dreading the ordeal. Why had he come to Texas, and why had he made friends with Gusten?

Dr. Monson and Mr. Bergman crouched down, level with Carl's bed. "Close your eyes," the doctor said, as he and

Mr. Bergman forced the bone into place. Pain shot through Carl's body as he bit down on the piece of wood.

"It's over," Dr. Monson said, perspiration dripping from his face. "I'm sorry if I hurt you."

Carl blinked, holding back tears. Mrs. Bergman came to the bed then and put a cold cloth on his head.

"I need some pieces of cotton and clean flour sacks," the doctor said to Mrs. Bergman.

When she gave the items to the doctor, he padded Carl's leg with cotton between the wooden splints. He then tore strips of cloth from flour sacks and wrapped them around Carl's leg to keep the splint in place.

Before he left, Dr. Monson patted Carl's arm. "Your leg will heal, but it will take time. Gusten will make you crutches from a strong tree limb. And remember to walk only on your good leg."

"Tack så mycket," Carl said in a weak voice.

Gusten was standing at the door with a frightened look on his face. "Does it hurt much?" Gusten asked.

"It hurt bad when the doctor set it. But it is better now."

"I'm glad," Gusten said with a sigh of relief.

"But I worry that Oscar will be angry. Will you ride to his farm and tell him what happened."

"Yes. And I'm sorry, Carl. I didn't want anything bad to happen to you."

"Just go tell my brother."

After Gusten left, Carl could not rest, thinking of Oscar's reaction to the accident. Would he be angry? Carl remembered his brother's warning: "Gusten's a wild sort."

Carl lay back in bed. He wanted to see his brother, but he dreaded his coming.

73

CHAPTER 11

Thanksgiving in Texas

As Carl lay on the bed, his leg aching, he wondered if his brother would really be angry with him.

He warned me about Gusten, but I didn't listen, Carl said to himself. *Now I'm hurt and in a foreign country, far from Mama and Papa. I hate Texas with its hot summer, rattlesnakes and grasshoppers. And a language I can't speak or understand. I wish I'd never left Sweden. I wish I had the money to return,* he thought.

Carl was still daydreaming when Lisa walked in, her blue eyes filled with compassion. "Here's a cup of water. Are you feeling better?"

"*Ja,* but I worry about what Oscar will say."

"He'll understand. It was just an accident. It was not your fault."

"I hope so," Carl replied, wishing he could confide in Lisa and tell her what really happened. But Gusten stood near the window, along with Mr. and Mrs. Bergman. Carl appreciated their help and didn't want to cause trouble.

"I hear Oscar coming now," Lisa said.

Carl looked up to see Oscar entering the room. He was

solemn, as usual. *Was he angry?* Carl wondered. Oscar came closer and put his arm around his brother's shoulder.

"Does it hurt?" he asked in a gentle voice.

"A little, but I'm feeling better. I worry about paying the doctor, though."

"We'll pay him a little at a time," Oscar replied.

Carl noticed Gusten staring out the window, his hands clasped tightly, almost as if he was praying. *What was wrong with him?* Carl wondered.

"My wagon is outside," Oscar said. "If you're ready, I'll carry you to the wagon and we can go home."

"He could stay with us until he gets his crutches," Mr. Bergman said.

"*Ja,* Lisa and Gusten would like the company," Mrs. Bergman added.

"Please stay," Gusten urged.

"Do you want to stay a few days?" Oscar asked him.

"*Ja,* if it is not too much trouble," Carl replied.

Oscar nodded and after a few minutes he left. Carl suddenly felt very tired. The Bergman family left so Carl could rest. Later, they tried their best to cheer him up.

"Mama made ginger cookies today. Want some?" Gusten asked.

"No, not now," Carl replied.

"I'll make your crutches after school tomorrow."

"Good, until then I'll just scoot or hop," Carl said, managing a small smile. "Maybe you could help me with my English while I'm here."

Gusten nodded. "I'll get my grammar book. But first we'll teach you words you must know."

Lisa helped by teaching him simple but important statements, such as "Good morning," "Thank you," "How much does it cost?"

Carl listened carefully, then repeated the statements. The language was not easy for him. But he promised himself he wouldn't give up. Someday he'd speak like the Americans.

Mrs. Bergman was usually in the room, listening as Carl

75

tried to master the language. She looked up one day with a frown on her face. "You need a real teacher, like Mrs. Lindell at the church," she said firmly.

"But Oscar says I don't have time to study," Carl replied.

"You do now," Gusten exclaimed, a big grin on his face. "You have time while your leg heals."

"But how would I get to the church?"

"I'll take you in the wagon after school," Gusten replied enthusiastically.

Carl's face brightened. "I'd like that."

Two days later, Gusten finished making crutches from tree limbs. When Carl first tried to use them, he almost fell. But in a few minutes, he was able to hobble across the floor.

How pleasant it was staying in the Bergman home, Carl thought. But he knew that Oscar and Ingrid were wondering when he'd come home.

"I should be going to Oscar's farm soon," he told Gusten.

"I'll take you whenever you want to go," Gusten promised.

The next afternoon Carl bid the Bergmans goodbye. *"Tack så mycket,"* he said clasping Mr. Bergman's hand and embracing Mrs. Bergman.

When he arrived back at the farm, Oscar and Ingrid seemed pleased to see him. Even little Erik clapped his hands.

"I'm sorry I can't do heavy work for awhile," Carl told his brother.

"I understand, *Bror.* I know you'll do what you can to help the homestead."

First thing the next day Carl began his new chores. He scraped corn from the cobs and fed it to the chickens. He churned butter for Ingrid, stirring the milk with a wooden paddle until it turned to creamy butter.

"We keep enough butter for ourselves but sell the rest. It helps buy the supplies we don't have," Ingrid explained.

When Carl finished his chores, he took his violin from its case. He had played it very little since he arrived in Texas.

He placed the fiddle under his chin and began to play *"Gardeblaten,"* a Swedish folksong. Hearing the lively sounds, Erik laughed and danced with delight.

On Wednesday Gusten came to take Carl to the English class. He met Mrs. Lindell, his teacher, a woman with strong, handsome features and eyes as blue as the Texas sky. She began to explain the language in a much clearer way than Lisa or Gusten had.

"Here's a grammar book with exercises you can do at home," she told Carl.

Carl felt self-conscious trying to pronounce the English sounds, but Mrs. Lindell encouraged him.

"You're doing quite well, Carl. Remember it will take a long time to master the English language. It is so different from Swedish."

"I have trouble with the 'j' sound, like in the boy's name, Joe," Carl said.

"Yes, 'j' in Swedish is pronounced like a 'y.' The 'th' sound is difficult, too. Put your tongue behind your front teeth to make that sound."

Carl nodded and tried to do as Mrs. Lindell suggested. But he was not too successful. She took a small chalkboard and wrote the word "horse." Next to that she wrote *"häst,"* the Swedish word for horse. Next she wrote "work" and *"arbeta"* beside it.

"Horse, work," Carl repeated several times.

At the end of the session, Carl felt as if he'd made a good start in learning English. "Could I borrow a math book, too?" he asked Mrs. Lindell.

"Certainly, keep it as long as you like," she replied.

Carl went to class every Wednesday and studied when he had free time. The little white church became his home away from home. He looked forward to his class and to talking with the friendly people on Sundays.

On the way back to the farm one Wednesday, he asked Gusten to do him a favor.

"If you see good pieces of cedar wood, would you bring them to me? I'd like to have them to carve animals."

Gusten laughed. "The woods are full of good cedar wood. I'll bring some next time I visit you."

When Gusten brought the cedar a few days later, Carl smelled the spicy scent of the wood and admired the red streak running through it. He took his knife and carved a rabbit. His experience working with wood at the spool factory served him well.

He gave his first carving, the rabbit, to Erik, who started to chew on it immediately. When Carl protested mildly, the boy began to cry. Carl conceded: "Go ahead, chew on it if you want. I can carve another."

He decided to give some of his carvings as Christmas gifts since he had no money to buy presents.

Carl's days were filled with household duties, his woodcarving, and fiddle playing. At times he still wished he could talk to Mama and Papa. When he missed them, he'd write them a letter.

Dear Mama and Papa,

I read your letter over and over. It was so good to hear from you. I had an accident riding a wild horse. I fell and broke my leg. But a Swedish doctor took good care of me and my leg is healing. The accident afforded me time to study English at the church with a good teacher, Mrs. Lindell. It is now November and still not even cold here. I think of you often and miss you.

Your son,
Carl

The November days gradually turned cooler and one afternoon Carl and Gusten were outdoors. They saw a flock of large birds flying very low to the ground.

"What kind of birds are those?" Carl asked.

"Wild turkeys. The Americans eat them for Thanksgiving."

"What is Thanksgiving?"

"It's a day when Americans give thanks for what they have and give a feast," Gusten explained. "The pilgrims first started it in 1621."

What interesting birds, Carl thought. Later, he drew a picture of a turkey to send to his sister, Axelina, in Sweden.

On Wednesday when Gusten arrived to take Carl to English class, he had a message from his parents. "They want all of you to eat Thanksgiving dinner with us. Will you come?"

Carl looked at Oscar and Ingrid, waiting for their replies. Ingrid smiled, pleased at the invitation. Even Oscar seemed happy.

"We would love to come," Ingrid said. "I'll bring a dessert."

"And I'll bring smoked sausage," Oscar added.

"Good, I'll tell Mama and Papa," Gusten said.

The days continued to grow cooler, and by the middle of November Carl helped Oscar make sausage from their slaughtered hogs. All the rest of the pork was placed in the smokehouse to save for the coming winter. Chicken and pork was all the meat they ever had.

On Thanksgiving morning Carl woke to see that the countryside had turned brown. The grass was now the color of straw.

"We had a freeze last night," Oscar explained. "It's finally time for cold weather."

"So different from Sweden," Carl commented.

They wore their Sunday clothes with their warm Swedish coats to the Bergman dinner. Carl knew that Oscar and Ingrid were excited about going to the Bergmans for dinner since they received few invitations like this.

"I made *ostkaka* for dessert," Ingrid said proudly. "But we will add blackberries that we picked last summer. There are no lingonberries in America."

When they got to the Bergman farm, Carl stepped carefully from the wagon with the aid of his crutch. Gusten watched from the porch.

"When will the doctor remove the splint?" he asked.

"Soon, maybe next week," Carl responded.

When Carl entered the dining room, he saw a table covered with a white linen cloth, good china and silver. It reminded him of his home in Sweden on special days.

The golden-brown turkey sat on a platter in the center of the table. The aroma of roasted meat filled the air. Other wonderful odors of mashed potatoes, beans, and baked bread filled the room. Carl's stomach growled.

Mr. Bergman carved the turkey, cutting off the drumsticks. Steam rose from the sweet potato casserole and swirled across the table. *What a feast,* Carl thought. He wished his parents in Sweden could enjoy such a meal.

The Bergmans and Olssons sat down and bowed their heads. Mr. Bergman blessed the food with a Swedish prayer: *"I Jesu namn till bords vi gå välsigna Gud den mat vi få,* in Jesus name to tables we go, God bless this food we receive."

Mr. Bergman piled each plate with generous helpings of turkey. Gusten saw to it that Carl received a drumstick. Carl stared at the meat, wondering how he should eat it. Should he use his hands or cut it with a knife?

Gusten watched mischievously as Carl tasted every other dish except the turkey. Carl spread fresh butter on his bread, then he looked at the others' plates. He saw no drumsticks.

"Don't you like turkey?" Gusten asked, grinning.

Carl's face turned pink. "I don't know how to eat it," he confessed.

Gusten laughed in his familiar manner. "Any way you want to," he said with a wink.

"Gusten, you're naughty, always teasing," Lisa scolded.

Carl took a bite of the drumstick and juice ran down his chin. He smiled and savored the rich flavor of the roasted bird.

When desserts were served later, Carl wondered if his stomach could hold another bite. "*Ostkaka,* rice pudding, ginger cookies, and prune whip," Lisa announced proudly.

Carl groaned but took a helping of each mouth-watering dessert. After dinner, Gusten turned to Carl. "Let's get some fresh air."

Outside Gusten walked quickly as Carl tried to keep up with him, using his crutches as poles to push himself. He felt truly carefree and happy. Then suddenly he lost his balance and fell on the rocky ground, landing on his injured leg.

"Are you hurt?" Gusten asked.

Carl fought back the tears and tried to get up. *Have I hurt my leg? Will I have to wear the cast weeks longer?* Carl worried.

"I'll get Papa," Gusten cried out.

Oscar and Mr. Bergman rushed to Carl's side and helped him to the house. As Carl lay on the bed, he felt like screaming in both anger and fear.

"We'll get Dr. Monson," Mrs. Bergman said.

"No need to bother him on Thanksgiving Day," Oscar said. "I'll take Carl to see him tomorrow."

Carl, Ingrid, Oscar, and Erik rode home in silence. The day that had begun with such joy had ended in gloom.

CHAPTER 12

A Texas Christmas

Carl spent a restless night, waking every few hours, wondering if he had reinjured his leg. He finally went to sleep and was snoring softly when Oscar nudged him.

"Wake up. We need to get to the doctor's office early before he gets busy."

Carl got up, poured a pitcher of water in the wash bowl and splashed it in his face. "My leg doesn't hurt. I don't need to see the doctor."

"We go," Oscar replied firmly. "It is time to see Dr. Monson."

"But the money? How can we pay? I've given him most of my savings."

"We will take butter and eggs to him today as a payment. We trade, or barter, like this in Texas. We give things we have in exchange for his help," Oscar explained.

A short while later, Carl climbed clumsily into the wagon. Before his recent fall, Carl had hoped the doctor would remove the splint from his leg. That would probably be impossible now and his leg would need to heal longer.

The morning had a chill to it as they rode against a

north wind. Only one other person was waiting in the office when they arrived.

"How is your leg?" Dr. Monson asked.

As Carl explained his fall, the doctor shook his head and frowned. He felt Carl's foot and toes. He then untied the flour sack strips to examine Carl's leg.

As the doctor gently removed the splint, Carl was almost afraid to look. He stared at his shriveled, very white leg.

"Move your foot, now your leg," the doctor said solemnly. He felt the area where the break had been. His bushy gray eyebrows moved up and down. His expression alarmed Carl and made him think the worst. Finally Dr. Monson smiled.

"Your leg is fine. You don't need to wear the splint. But walk slowly at first and not too long at one time. The muscles must regain their strength."

Carl grabbed the doctor's hand. *"Tack så mycket,"* he said over and over. *I'm the luckiest boy in Texas,* he thought.

"Don't ride any more wild horses," the doctor warned.

Oscar nodded. "He's a farmer, not a cowboy. Will you take these eggs and butter as part of what we owe?" he asked, handing the doctor a basket.

"Of course, and I like plump chickens, too," the doctor said, a smile behind his beard.

Carl shook the doctor's hand and the brothers returned to the farm.

The next day Carl was pleasantly surprised by the strength in his leg. He was able to resume most of his farm chores. After a day of work, he took a piece of spicy-scented cedar in his hand and began carving a bird to give his sister for Christmas.

As he thought about Christmas, he felt homesick. He couldn't imagine the holidays without his parents and the snowy countryside of Sweden. But later as he heard Ingrid talk of Christmas preparations, he got excited.

"Mrs. Bergman said that the store has dried lutfisk now," Ingrid said.

"Herring, too?" Carl asked, and Ingrid nodded.

His mouth watered at the thought of pickled herring.

Perhaps his first Christmas in Texas would not be as bad as he thought.

"I'm busy smoking pork. Carl, you take the wagon to town and buy the lutfisk and herring," Oscar said.

"But I don't speak English well enough," Carl said.

"You can buy lutfisk and herring. You won't have to speak much," Oscar insisted.

Carl considered this. He didn't want to go, but he did want to enjoy the white fish on Christmas Eve even if the lutfisk did smell bad when it was cooking. He hitched the mules and started to town.

The store was crowded as people waited to buy supplies. Carl looked at cowboy boots first, wondering how much a pair might cost.

"Hey, Swede," a teenage boy called out, then said something in English which Carl could not understand. Carl started to walk away but two boys followed him, their voices harsh and unfriendly.

When he got to the counter, the owner looked at the American boys and frowned. "Leave him alone, boys," he said. "You want lutfisk and herring?" the man asked Carl.

"*Ja,*" Carl said solemnly.

The owner got the two kinds of fish and handed them to Carl who paid for them quickly. His face felt hot and his palms sweaty. The Americans boys still lurked nearby.

Outside, the boys taunted him again and tried to grab the package of fish. "Dumb Swede," they shouted.

Humiliated, Carl clutched the fish, got into the wagon and drove the team of mules as fast as he could. Back at the farm, he unhitched the mules and went inside.

"So?" Oscar asked. "Did you have any trouble?"

"No," Carl answered without looking at his brother.

On December 13 Ingrid made sweet rolls and hot coffee early in the morning. "We have no daughter to serve us on this special Lucia Day, but we remember our custom."

Carl recalled that each December 13 in Sweden his sister, Christina, rose at dawn, made breakfast and sang the Lucia song to his parents. How he missed Christina.

"Play your fiddle for us," Ingrid said. "I heard you practicing *'Tre Pepparkakagubbar.'*"

"Ja, play the song," Oscar urged, the spirit of Christmas in his voice.

The family sang the humorous song of the three gingerbread men as little Erik danced around them.

"Today is the day I start preparing the lutfisk," Ingrid said, after the celebration.

Carl helped her fill a gallon jug of water and watched as she added a teaspoon of lye and poured the mixture over the dried fish. Each day for nine days she poured out the mixture, then added fresh water and lye.

Carl and Oscar put ham and sausage in the small shed they called the smokehouse. The smoked meat would keep a long time without spoiling.

As the days passed and Christmas drew near, Carl thought more and more about his family in Sweden. Then a letter arrived from Christina.

Dear Brothers and Ingrid,

I am so close to you yet so far. Twenty-five miles seems a great distance. I had no money for a train ticket. But I have good news. The Littletons, my employers, are leaving town for Christmas. They told me I could visit you in Brushy at that time and are buying my train ticket. I hope I will not crowd you. I am so excited. And I'm still learning English. Are you, Carl?
Lovingly,
Christina

"Such good news," Carl exclaimed. "We will be together at Christmas. I'm sure Henning will come, too."

He'd tell his sister about his English class and say a few words to her. Of course, he didn't feel as if he could speak with the Americans yet, but he was learning. He knew this was his only chance to learn to speak and write in English. And become an American.

Christina arrived on December 22, two days before Christmas Eve. "I've missed all of you so much," she said, embracing Carl. "Life is different in a city. I long for country living."

"Your clothes are fine," Ingrid said, touching the soft velvet of Christina's dress, then feeling the coarseness of her own.

"The Littletons treat me well, but it's not the same as being with family. I look forward to the day when Henning and I can marry and live close to you."

"Henning will be here on Christmas Eve," Carl said.

Christina's eyes brightened at the thought of her boyfriend. That night Carl gave his sister his bed and he slept on a pallet on the floor. He secretly continued carving his wooden figures to give as Christmas gifts.

The day before Christmas Eve he and Oscar walked to the woods to cut the cedar tree. It was the one that Carl had admired for so long. He could hardly wait to decorate it.

"Tree," Erik said. "*Jultomten* come."

"The *jultomten* comes to good little boys," Carl said, remembering what his father told him many years ago. He knew that the Americans called the Christmas elf, Santa Claus. "Me good boy," Erik said.

Ingrid and Christina spent the next day baking Swedish rye and eggtwist bread. The wonderful odors of bread baking kept Carl constantly hungry.

Carl rose early on December 24. Christmas Eve was the day he and his family reserved for their special celebration. Henning arrived at mid-morning and greeted Christina with a kiss on the cheek. Carl looked on as her face flushed with happiness.

He smelled the spicy scent of sausage as it floated in the thick soup that Ingrid had made. He looked in the pot at the colorful vegetables and ham.

"*Dopp i gryta,*" Oscar said. "We do this to remember those times in Sweden when the only food was dark bread and thin broth."

Carl dipped his bread in the broth, knowing that Mama, Papa, and the rest of the family would be repeating the same ritual in Sweden on this day.

"Light the candles on the tree, Carl," Oscar said.

As Carl did so, the cedar tree decorated with strands of popcorn and cranberries lit up the entire house. Carl thought it had to be the most beautiful tree he'd ever seen. Little Erik's eyes widened as the candles glowed. The presents under the tree were wrapped in wrinkled paper saved from another Christmas.

Wearing a red cap, Henning played the role of the *jultomten*, giving out the gifts. "Have you been a good boy?" he asked Erik.

"*Ja*, good boy." Erik said as he unwrapped Carl's gift to him. "It's a wooden ship like the one that brought me to America," Carl told the boy.

Christina handed Carl the warm cap she had knitted for him, and Carl gave her the carving of a mockingbird, the state bird of Texas. He had managed to buy Ingrid a small amount of peppermints. Ingrid gave him the new shirt she had made. *What a wonderful Christmas,* Carl thought. Not having Mama and Papa with them was the only sad part.

He watched his sister's face as she and Henning exchanged small gifts. How happy they seemed.

That evening Ingrid served the big meal with the main course, lutfisk, which had taken weeks of preparation. Carl knew it wouldn't seem like Christmas without the fish. But he wasn't excited about the smell that lingered in the house.

"Put some gravy on the lutfisk," Ingrid urged, passing the white milk gravy to Carl. He helped himself to boiled potatoes, beets and the special treat, lingonberries.

"I never thought Mama and Papa could send us lingonberries for Christmas," Carl said to his sister.

She nodded, savoring the tart flavor of the berries. She ate slowly, enjoying the Christmas feast.

When the meal was finished, Ingrid placed a bowl of sweetened rice with a cinnamon stick in the middle on the table.

"Rice pudding," Carl exclaimed.

"Remember, I hid one almond in the pudding, and the

person who gets the almond will be married during the year," Ingrid announced.

Carl looked at his sister and smiled. Christina waited until everyone had taken a helping of the pudding. Carl ate his quickly but he didn't find an almond.

Oscar, Henning, and Ingrid began to eat their pudding but they also found nothing. Everyone stared at Christina.

She took a helping of the pudding and slowly brought a spoonful to her mouth. Carl watched carefully from the corner of his eyes and saw her smile.

"I got the almond," she said proudly.

"So Christina will be married within the year," Carl said. "I hope she marries you, Henning," he teased.

"I hope so, too," Henning said, blushing. "And now I must be going if I'm to attend *Julotta* at five o'clock tomorrow morning."

Carl fell asleep not long after Henning left. It was still dark the next morning when he heard noises in the kitchen. The smell of coffee helped him wake up.

He was glad to have his heavy Swedish clothes on this cold morning. He went to the outdoor privy that served as the family toilet, then returned, shivering. He lit the kerosene lamp in the dark room, and he felt more awake.

When Carl walked in the kitchen, he saw Oscar, Ingrid, and Christina eating bread and butter and sipping coffee. Erik sat in his father's lap.

"It's almost time to hitch the mules to the wagon and go to church," Oscar said as Carl sat down and helped himself to bread and butter.

A few minutes later, the family climbed in the wagon for the dark ride down the dirt road to church. Erik was snuggled between Carl and Christina. Carl's violin case lay across his knees. As they neared the church, he saw the windows glowing brightly from the candlelight.

Inside the church, Ruth Nilsson was playing the pump organ, her feet moving up and down on the pedals. The old hymn, "Be Greeted This Happy Morning" echoed through the church.

Carl walked to the front of the church, violin in hand.

Placing it under his chin, he played "Hosianna, David's Son," the traditional Swedish hymn. Pastor Lundquist then gave the Christmas sermon and more singing followed.

"Children, come receive your Christmas fruit," the pastor said at the end of the service.

Erik proudly took his apple. He was smiling from ear to ear.

As the candles blazed in the little church, friends greeted each other.

"God Jul," Carl told Gusten, handing him a wooden horse carving. He gave a bird to Lisa, and she gave him a pair of hand-knitted socks.

"Come see us soon," Gusten told Carl as they left.

The sun was beginning to rise as the family rode back to the farm. Carl was quiet, thinking of his family in Sweden.

"I hope someday that Mama and Papa can be with us," he said finally.

"I pray they will," Christina said.

Inside the house the smell of eggs and sausage filled every room. Carl ate hungrily, warming himself by the wood stove. He loved the kitchen — the warmest room in the house.

Carl took a walk after breakfast, exploring the woods beyond the farm. The dark green trees reminded him of Sweden. He thought of the day, his first Christmas in Texas. Such dreams he had. *Would they all come true?* he wondered.

The next morning Christina packed her few belongings to return to Austin. The happiness had left her face as she told everyone goodbye.

"I won't return until late spring, just in time for my wedding," she told Carl.

He nodded, then drove her in the wagon to the depot where Henning waited. Carl watched from a distance as his sister and her boyfriend held hands, then kissed briefly.

She boarded the train and waved as it began to move down the track.

"Goodbye!" Carl called out.

CHAPTER 13

Trouble on the Farm

January arrived with a blast of cold air from the north. Carl shivered, realizing he had become accustomed to the warm climate of Texas.

"In winter we mend fences, fix harnesses, and catch up on other chores," Oscar reminded him. "And we let the fields rest."

Carl liked the idea of "letting the fields rest." It was nature's way of restoring the land. He looked at the field and saw the remains of cotton and corn stalks they had plowed under.

One day Carl walked several miles to Dr. Monson's office with two cleaned chickens wrapped in a flour sack and a loaf of Ingrid's brown bread in a basket.

"Payment for fixing my leg," Carl told the doctor.

"Ah, nice plump hens, just the way I like them. And good Swedish bread. You've paid your bill in full," Dr. Monson said.

Carl smiled and shook the doctor's hand. *"Tack så mycket."*

Later that day, at Oscar's farm, they faced the hard job of mending fences. Carl had never seen barbed wire in Sweden. As he stretched the wire tightly, Oscar nailed it to the cedar posts. The sharp points pricked Carl's fingers, making them bleed.

With the cold weather came the need for more firewood. Carl and Oscar spent hours cutting limbs and splitting logs to burn for warmth in the house.

"We never have enough wood to burn or meat to eat in winter," Oscar said. "That's the reason we're curing pork in the smokehouse."

They did what work they could do despite the weather. Carl helped Ingrid make soap from lye and the oil left from slaughtering hogs. He also worked for his American neighbors on Saturdays. Each time he worked, he earned fifty or seventy-five cents. He saved the money in the little box he kept under his bed.

Gusten came by one afternoon. "Get on my horse with me. I want to show you something," he said.

A mile down the road Gusten brought Smokey, his horse, to a halt. "Look," he said, pointing to a roan, or reddish-colored horse in the pasture. "See that mare. I think the farmer will sell her."

"For how much?" Carl asked, trying not to get his hopes up.

"Probably $15 or less. He doesn't need the horse. She's old but healthy and good-natured."

Carl watched the horse trot around the pasture. She held her head high; her body seemed muscular. "I'd really like to buy her." Carl said longingly.

The owner of the horse appeared, wanting to know why the boys were there. "My friend wants to buy your horse. Will you sell her for $12?" Gusten asked.

The farmer frowned. "She's worth $20, but I'll consider $15," he replied.

"Thanks, we'll be back," Gusten said. "I think you have a deal," he added as they rode away.

"I still need about $1.50," Carl said.

Back at Oscar's farm, Carl made sure he did his share of the chores so his brother wouldn't complain. He rushed to finish everything before his Wednesday English class at the church.

"You're making fast progress," Mrs. Lindell told him that Wednesday.

"I brought you this," Carl said, handing her a carving of a cardinal bird.

"It's beautiful; you have a talent for carving," she said feeling the smoothness of the reddish wood with its spicy odor. "Have you thought of selling your work?"

Carl laughed. "Who would buy them?"

"Every first Monday of the month people sell items on the square in Georgetown. You should take your carvings and see if they'll sell. First Monday is next week. I plan to sell knitted caps the ladies of the church made. I'll see you there."

Carl really didn't believe Mrs. Lindell. Why would anyone pay money for his wooden figures? But he took her advice and went to the square. He had never seen so many people at one time. They were all buying and selling.

Carl put his carvings beside some handmade quilts and waited. Homemade bread and cakes were for sale; knitted caps and scarves, even chickens in pens waited for buyers. He watched nervously as the townspeople inspected the goods. Nobody seemed interested in his carvings. Then a well-dressed woman stopped and picked up a wooden bird.

"Did you carve this, young man?" she asked.

Carl understood the question and replied, "Yes."

"I'll pay you $1.50 for all ten figures. I live in Austin, and I can sell them at my shop. I may be back next month. Do you have others?"

Carl nodded, not completely sure he understood her meaning. Mrs. Lindell who happened to be near, smiled in approval.

"She'll pay you for these and buy more next time," Mrs. Lindell said in Swedish.

Carl took the money, amazed at his good fortune. "Thank you," he said in English.

After the woman walked away, he turned to Mrs. Lindell. "It would take me two days of hard work to earn this much."

Mrs. Lindell laughed and patted Carl's arm. "I told you someone would buy your carvings. You have a gift for carving."

"I'm grateful to you for suggesting that I sell my carvings. But I must get back to the farm. Oscar needs me," Carl said to Mrs. Lindell.

"I must leave now, too. I'd like to ride with you to my farm."

The wind blew in their faces as the wagon chugged along the bumpy road. They passed a large, white stone building, different from any Carl had seen in Georgetown.

A tower, shaped like a church steeple, extended from the top of the building. Carl stared at the dignified structure.

"I don't remember this building," he said.

"It's Southwestern University. Students go there to study and learn," she replied.

"What do they study?"

"All kinds of things — math, literature, music, science, and religion," she answered.

"It looks like a wonderful place to study," Carl said.

"It is. Perhaps you'll be able to go there someday. The university has hundreds of books and many good teachers, too."

Carl admired the building. Would it really be possible for him to study there? He paused in front of the structure, deep in thought.

"You can be almost anything you want to be in Texas," Mrs. Lindell said.

"I know. I have lots of dreams inside me."

After he left Mrs. Lindell at her farm, Carl hurried to Oscar's. He emptied the money from his pockets and placed it in the box under his bed. He had enough to buy a horse now. He would tell Gusten soon and he could buy his horse.

He saw Oscar coming in from the outside. "Do you want me to do any chores?" Carl asked.

"First, you should read this letter from Mama and Papa," Oscar replied.

Dear Oscar, Carl and Ingrid,

Sweden has had a bitter-cold winter. Little Axelina has been very sick most of the time. And we have many more months of cold weather ahead of us. We think about you often and try to imagine what Texas is like. Recently we made an important decision. We cannot remain in Sweden much longer. The food is scarcer now. We don't even have enough potatoes to eat. We plan to sell our furniture and some farm tools. The money we receive plus a little we've saved will bring us to Texas. That is, if we can live with you for awhile. I know we are asking a lot, but we must come. It's good to know that we have two, prosperous sons in Texas who can help us. Please let us know what you think of our plan. We would arrive in early summer.

With love,
Mama and Papa

Carl's face broke into a big smile. "I can't believe they're really coming. I didn't expect them so soon."

"It is good news," Oscar replied, his voice flat and without feeling.

"What is the matter? You don't seem glad."

"I am, *Bror,* but where will they live? We have no room for them in this house."

"We can build a new room to the house. I am good at building. I know I can do it."

"Lumber and nails cost money. I must tell you my secret. After I received payment for the cotton, I bought more land. I don't have any money for lumber." Oscar confessed.

"Will it take so much money?"

"Yes, it will take money, that I don't have. Mama and Papa will have to wait to come. After harvest, next autumn, we can buy lumber and build a room."

"But that might be October or even as late as December. Sweden is already cold by that time. And the trip on the ocean would be bad for Axelina."

Oscar shrugged. "I don't see any other solution. They will have to wait until next winter."

Carl stared out the window, watching the wind blow the leaves on the ground. How could they tell Mama and Papa not to come?

"I'm going to take a walk," Carl said solemnly.

The north wind blew in his face as he walked through the barren fields. *How could Oscar have spent all the money,* he wondered. He had worked hard for Oscar, but he didn't understand his brother. There wasn't enough money to buy lumber, and Mama and Papa could not come.

He went back inside to his little room. No, it was not big enough for him, his parents, and Axelina. He took the money box from under the bed and counted.

He counted nickels, dimes, quarters, and a few dollars. The sum came to $15.75, enough to buy a horse. Or enough to buy lumber to build a room for Mama and Papa.

Carl put the money back, sliding the box under the bed. Then he went to the kitchen to tell Oscar what was on his mind.

"I can spend the money I've been saving for a horse on lumber for the new room," he said in a sure voice.

Oscar stared at him. "I know what the horse means to you and how hard you've worked to save the money."

"I want to spend my money on lumber. There's nothing more to talk about. Someday I'll get a horse. But not now."

Oscar put his hand on his brother's shoulder. "It's very good of you, Carl. I wish I could help more."

"I've made up my mind. Now, I must get busy. The weather is getting colder. I'll check on the meat in the smokehouse and bring in more buckets of water before dark," Carl said.

"*Ja,* we need more water," Oscar said, coughing.

"Are you catching a cold?"

"It's just the weather. When a cold front moves in, they call it a 'blue norther' in Texas."

Oscar had another coughing spell and couldn't speak. Carl went outside to finish the chores.

The weather turned even colder that night. When Carl awoke the next day, he saw sleet falling. A light snow then fell. He looked outside and seeing the ground covered with white, he smiled.

Carl was reminded of Sweden. He remembered the fun he had throwing snowballs and bobsledding with his friends. The sun went down early that afternoon as snow-clouds hovered above. Oscar was tending the mules as Carl lit the kerosene lamp and put more wood on the fire. Keeping enough wood cut took constant work. The stove devoured it like a hungry animal.

Ingrid came up to Carl with a worried look on her face.

"Where is Oscar? He should be finished with chores by now," Ingrid said in a concerned voice.

"He's tending the mules," Carl replied. "I'll go see if I can help him."

The soft snow gently pelted Carl's face as he walked to the barn. He saw Oscar covering the mules with old blankets.

"I'll finish here, *Bror*," Carl said.

Oscar began coughing. He couldn't speak but nodded his head at Carl's offer to finish with the animals. His teeth chattered and he stumbled as he tried to walk.

"Wait, I'll help you to the house," Carl told him.

Carl finished giving the mules pitchforks of hay, then led Oscar to the house. His brother shivered and coughed, as he tried to get inside. His face was red and raw from the cold.

Ingrid helped Oscar get to bed, covering him with quilts and blankets. The next day Oscar couldn't get out of bed. He burned with fever, and his body ached. Carl sat with him, putting cool cloths on his face and listening to his delirious ramblings.

"Papa fell in the snow. We must find him," Oscar mumbled in his dazed state.

"No, we are in Texas. Papa is in Sweden," Carl reminded his brother.

"What shall we do, Carl?" Ingrid asked in alarm.

"I will get Dr. Monson," Carl suggested, remembering the good doctor.

"You can't go in this weather," Ingrid said as the north wind blew snow over the fields. "We have to wait."

Ingrid made broth from boiling a chicken. She tried to feed it to Oscar, but he refused to eat. She placed a mustard plaster over his chest and kept him covered constantly.

The storm continued to rage. Oscar remained very sick. He burned with fever, then shivered with cold.

When Oscar's body shook from coughing, Carl felt his brother's pain. And when Oscar didn't speak for two days, Carl knew that his brother might die. Both Carl and Ingrid shared the same fear. What would happen to the farm, and what would happen to all of them if Oscar died? Carl sat up with him that night, sometimes afraid that his brother had stopped breathing.

On the third day the snow stopped falling as nature ended her tirade. A strange calm fell over the countryside. That morning, miraculously, Oscar opened his eyes.

"What happened to me?" he asked, confused.

"You were very sick, but you will get well now," Carl told him. "Try to drink a little broth."

He spooned warm soup down his brother's throat, waiting patiently for him to swallow.

"The worst is over," Carl assured his brother. "You will feel better soon."

"I must depend on you now," Oscar said weakly.

"Don't worry. I'm strong. Just get well."

The next week Carl worked very hard, cutting wood, milking cows, getting buckets of water to the house. But he was glad to help his brother and make up for the weeks when he couldn't work because of his broken leg.

Oscar's strength returned slowly. He could walk and gather eggs but he couldn't do much work. One day he turned to Carl and spoke in a firm voice.

"Our supplies are almost gone. We need flour, sugar, coffee, and salt. I'm too weak to go to town. You must go to the store for us, Carl."

"But I don't speak English well enough. The owner might cheat me."

"No, the owner is an honest man. And you speak enough English to buy our supplies. You must believe in yourself."

Carl sat quietly for a few minutes. Fear of failure haunted him. Would people make fun of him? Could he really make the purchases?

Oscar looked at him, waiting for a reply.

CHAPTER 14

"You can be anything you want to be in Texas."

Carl knew what he had to do. The next morning he put on his warm Swedish coat and cap and left to gather eggs in the hen house. Ingrid took the eggs and packed them carefully between layers of hay in an empty molasses bucket.

She wrapped the cold butter in a clean flour sack and handed it and the eggs to Carl. "You will barter, or trade, the eggs and butter for part of our supplies," she said.

Carl nodded, hoping he could speak enough English to barter with the store owner. Oscar gave him two dollars for the supplies. Carl then hitched the mules to the wagon and headed for Georgetown.

On the way, he practiced saying English words and sounds. He hoped he could remember all the sentences and words that Mrs. Lindell had taught him.

Saturday was busy on the square in Georgetown. Horses tied to hitching posts with wagons waited patiently in front of the store. People smiled and greeted each other as they went in and out of the store.

Carl tied his mules to the post and patted their necks. He squared his shoulders and climbed the steps to the general store, silent and alone.

Inside the store he placed the bucket of eggs and loaf of butter carefully on the counter. "I am Carl Olsson, brother of Oscar," he said to the owner, Mr. Allen.

"Yes, I remember you. Where is Oscar?" Mr. Allen asked.

"Very sick," Carl replied.

"I'm sorry to hear that. I see that you have butter and eggs to barter. You can shop while I count and candle the eggs."

Mr. Allen held each egg beside a lighted candle to see inside and test the freshness. Carl watched a few minutes, then walked around the store.

He picked up a large sack of flour and a sack of sugar. He scooped up green coffee beans, emptying them into a can. Then Carl saw a bucket of molasses and put it on the counter. He placed a sack of salt beside it, hoping he had enough money. The peppermints for Ingrid would have to wait.

He looked anxiously at Mr. Allen, then at the items he needed to buy. What if he didn't have enough money? Mr. Allen looked up at him and smiled.

"Don't look so worried, Carl. We'll work everything out," he said.

Carl's muscles relaxed as he took a long, deep breath. Mr. Allen weighed the sacks and wrote the cost on a piece of paper. He then figured the credit for eggs and butter, subtracting it from the total.

"You have $1.50 credit for the butter and eggs, Carl. And your purchases total $3.40. You owe $1.90. I'll throw in the peppermints for free."

Carl's frown changed into a smile as he fished out the crumpled dollar bills. He handed them to Mr. Allen, who gave him a dime in change.

"You figured the amount perfectly, Carl."

Carl smiled, then said "Thank you."

"Thanks for shopping today. I know you'll be a good citizen in Texas. You'll have a farm of your own someday."

"I will, yes," Carl replied.

Mr. Allen shook his hand and smiled broadly.

Carl held his head high as he walked out into the cold wind. He had done well, he knew. He had talked to Mr. Allen in English, and he succeeded in buying and bartering.

As he walked to the wagon, he saw the group of boys who once teased him about his language. One of the boys recognized Carl.

"Hey, Swede, remember me?"

"Yes," Carl said, his eyes straight ahead.

"Then say my name."

The other boys surrounded Carl, preventing him from walking further. "Say his name," one taunted.

"Yeah, Swede, cat got your tongue? What's his name?"

Carl knew the boys wanted to hear him mispronounce the name, "Joe." He had practiced it over and over, but with the boys staring at him, he felt unsure of himself.

He wanted to walk through the barrier of bodies and get away from the boys. But they surrounded him in a threatening circle. He sucked in his breath and hoped he could say the word "Joe."

"Name is Joe," Carl said slowly using the correct sound for "j."

"The Swede knows English now!" one of the boys exclaimed.

Carl understood the boy's words. When the teenager smiled at him, Carl returned the smile, a gesture of friendship. The American boy respected him now. The suspicious looks on the others' faces disappeared as their circle broke, giving Carl the freedom to leave.

"Goodbye and good luck," the first boy said.

"Goodbye," Carl replied with a new confidence in his voice.

As he made his way to the wagon, the sacks weighed heavy in his arms. But he didn't mind. He felt nine feet tall. He had actually talked to the American boys, and they hadn't laughed at him. They had even smiled. Perhaps someday they would really be his friends.

"Giddap," he shouted at the mules, as they began pulling the wagon.

He passed the pasture where the reddish horse grazed, the one he had wanted to buy. The horse trotted to the fence as Carl took a good look at her, knowing now that she would not belong to him. She would have been a good horse, but the timing was wrong. There would be other horses, he mused.

When he came to Oscar's farm, he drove the wagon down the dirt road. Seeing Oscar standing in the doorway of the house, Carl shouted, "Yahoo!"

Oscar had a puzzled look on his face. "Did you get everything we need? And did the owner treat you with respect?"

"*Ja*, and I spoke good English. I bartered and bought supplies," Carl replied proudly.

"I'm proud of you, *Bror*. I couldn't have managed without you the past few weeks. You've been a big help to Ingrid and me. We're glad you came to live with us."

Carl stared at his brother, surprised at such warm feelings. "It seems like such a long time since I left Sweden. So much has happened to me. But I'm beginning to like this wild state."

"Texas is not so bad. Think of the rich land, the warm rains that make crops grow, and the tall plants bulging with cotton at harvest," Oscar said.

Carl nodded. "I'll always miss Sweden. I'll always dream of its lakes and its snowy countryside. But I'm glad I came here. I know that Mama and Papa will like Texas."

"Giving up the horse you wanted was a brave act."

"I can wait for my horse. Other things are more important now."

Carl looked at the farm and saw green shoots of grass peeking from the soil. A robin perched in an oak tree. He couldn't help smiling, knowing spring was on the way.

With a new season, came new life. The future looked bright. He and Papa might buy a farm. He could go to school again. *There is so much to learn*, he thought.

He remembered what Mrs. Lindell had said: "You can be anything you want to be in Texas."

Main street of Georgetown. Horse-drawn wagons loaded with cotton bales. A. J. Nelson taking crop to market.
— Institute of Texan Cultures, Estate of Thomas E. Nelson

Cotton Gin at New Sweden. Adolph Anderson stands on platform under scale where cotton was weighed. Early 1800s.
— Institute of Texan Cultures, Beatrice Olson

Wash day in Brushy with iron pots. Lovina Blom and Esther Blom on a farm near Georgetown.

— Institute of Texan Cultures, Dana Noren

Cattle crossing the river.

— Barker History Center

Boy driving wagon with mules on cotton farm in Williamson County. (Boy is Gottfried Swenson.)

— Institute of Texan Cultures, Charlene Jordan

Swedish Methodist Church at Brushy, early 1880s. Many new immigrants attended this church.

— Georgetown Heritage Society

First Monday in Georgetown, an important day to buy and sell in the town square.

— Georgetown Heritage Society

Williamson County Courthouse, early 1800s.
— Georgetown Heritage Society

Southwestern University building.
— Georgetown Heritage Society

Glossary of Swedish Words & Sayings

arbeta	work
bror	brother
dopp i gryta	dip in the broth
fabrik	factory
flicka	girl
främmande	foreigner
"Gardeblaten"	Swedish folksong
god morgon	good morning
god Jul	Merry Christmas
häst	horse
hej	hello
hurra	hurrah
ja	yes
julgran	Christmas tree
julotta	church service early Christmas morning
jultomten	Christmas elf who brings presents
kompis	friend
limpa	rye bread
lutfisk	white fish from Sweden
Midsommer	day in late June when sun never sets in Sweden
mjolk	milk
mormor	grandma
ostkaka	Swedish custard dessert
pepparkaka	ginger cookies
pojke	boy
"Sköna Maj Välkommen"	"Beautiful May Welcome"

smörgåsbord	bread, butter, and other foods
studerande	student
Sverige	Sweden
tack så mycket	thank you
"Tre Pepparkakagubbar"	"Three Gingerbread Men"
vacker	beautiful
Välkommen	welcome

Bibliography

Barton, H. Arnold. *Letters From the Promised Land, Swedes in America, 1840–1914.* Minnesota: University of Minneapolis, 1973.

Hillbrand, Percie V. *The Swedes in America.* Minneapolis: Lerner, 1966.

Lorenzen, Lilly. *Of Swedish Ways.* New York: Gramercy Press, Dillon, 1986.

Lindquist, Willis. "Life's Flavor on a Swedish Farm," from "Rocky Hills of Småland Thousands of Sturdy Citizens Have Emigrated to United States." *National Geographic,* p. 393–414. September 1939.

Lubbock, Francis. *Six Decades in Texas, Memories of Francis Lubbock, 1861–1863.* B.C. Jones and Company, Editor: C. W. Raines: Austin, 1900.

Moberg, Vilhelm. *Unto a Good Land.* Translated by Gustaf Lannestock. New York: Simon and Shuster, 1951.

Nelson, Helge. *The Swedes and the Swedish Settlements in America.* New York, 1943.

Palm, Rufus A., Jr. *The Arrival of the Palms in Texas,* typescript in the Barker Texas History Center, Austin, 1976.

Purcell, Mabelle and Purcell, Stuart and others. *This is Texas.* Austin: L. P. Hawkins, 1977.

Rosenquist, C. M. "The Swedes of Texas." *American Swedish Historical Yearbook,* 1945.

Saint John's Methodist Church, Georgetown, Texas. *A History 1882–1982 Centennial Celebration.* Georgetown, 1982.

Scarbrough, Clara. *Land of Good Water: A Williamson County Texas History.* Georgetown, Texas: Williamson County Sun Publishers, 1973.

Scott, Larry E. *The Swedish Texans.* San Antonio: University of

Texas, Institute of Texan Cultures, 1990.

Severin, Ernest. *Svenskarn i Texas ord och Bild 1838–1918.* Austin: E. L. Steck, 1919.

Sichel, Marion. *Scandinavia.* New York: Chelsea, 1987.

Swenson, Johannes. *Journey to Texas in 1867.* Translated by Carl Widen. Reprinted for *The Southwestern Historical Quarterly,* Vol. LXII, July 1958.

Whisenhunt, Donald W. *Texas – A Sesquicentennial Celebration.* Austin: Eakin Press, 1984.